THE QUENTARIS CHRONICLES

Quentaris in Flames, Michael Pryor
Swords of Quentaris, Paul Collins
The Perfect Princess, Jenny Pausacker
The Revognase, Lucy Sussex
Beneath Quentaris, Michael Pryor
Slaves of Quentaris, Paul Collins
Stones of Quentaris, Michael Pryor
Dragonlords of Quentaris, Paul Collins
Angel Fever, Isobelle Carmody
The Ancient Hero, Sean McMullen
The Mind Master, John Heffernan
Treasure Hunters of Quentaris, Margo Lanagan
Rifts through Quentaris, Karen R. Brooks
The Plague of Quentaris, Gary Crew
The Cat Dreamer, Isobelle Carmody
Princess of Shadows, Paul Collins
Nightmare in Quentaris, Michael Pryor
The Murderers' Apprentice, Pamela Freeman
Stolen Children of Quentaris, Gary Crew
Stars of Quentaris, Michael Pryor
Pirates of Quentaris, Sherryl Clark
The Forgotten Prince, Paul Collins
Prisoner of Quentaris, Anna Ciddor
The Skyflower, Justin D'Ath

The Skyflower

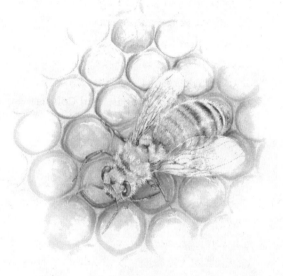

Justin D'Ath

Series editors: Michael Pryor and Paul Collins

Lothian
BOOKS

For Ryn, who gifted me the bee girl.

Lothian Books
An imprint of Hachette Livre Australia
132 Albert Road, South Melbourne, Victoria 3205
www.lothian.com.au

First published 2006

National Library of Australia
Cataloguing-in-Publication data:

D'Ath, Justin.
The skyflower

For children.
ISBN 0 7344 0933 8.

1. Life on other planets — Juvenile fiction. 2. Quests (Expeditions) —
Juvenile fiction. 3. Magic — Juvenile fiction. I. Pryor, Michael. II. Collins,
Paul. III. Title. (Series: Quentaris chronicles).

A823.3

Cover artwork by Jeremy Reston
Map by Jeremy Maitland-Smith
Original map by Marc McBride
Cover and text design by John van Loon
Printed in Australia by Griffin Press

Contents

1	*Fight! Fight! Fight!*	9
2	The Bee Girl	19
3	A Disgrace to the Family Name	26
4	The Green Petal	33
5	Deadly Cave	39
6	I Hope the Zolka Get You!	49
7	The Monster	55
8	Sword-for-hire	62
9	World of Giants	68
10	The Hectapus	75
11	The Garden in the Sky	83
12	Too Close for Comfort	88
13	Blood!	95
14	Chasing *it*	99
15	Not Th-o Tough	107
16	A Good Fairytale	114
17	*So* Brave!	123
18	Run!	130
19	Goodbye Kiss	135
20	Quentaris's Most Wanted	144
21	The Seed	154

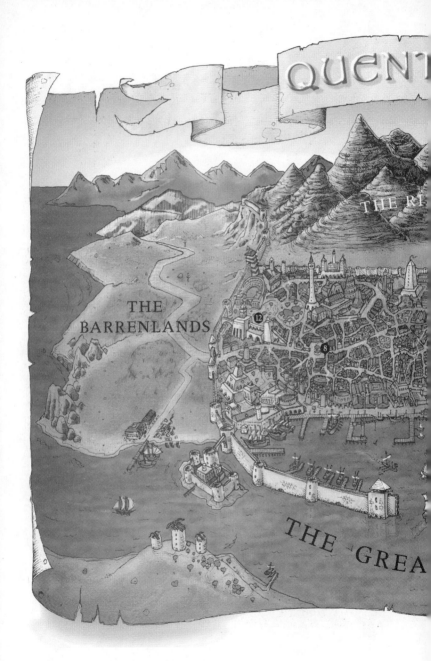

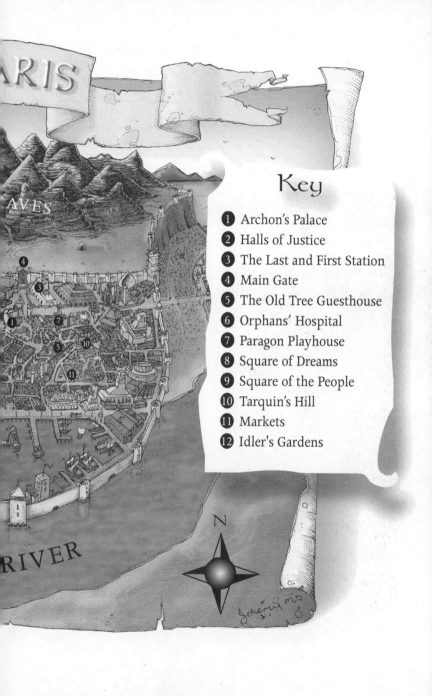

...ARIS

AVES

Key

1 Archon's Palace
2 Halls of Justice
3 The Last and First Station
4 Main Gate
5 The Old Tree Guesthouse
6 Orphans' Hospital
7 Paragon Playhouse
8 Square of Dreams
9 Square of the People
10 Tarquin's Hill
11 Markets
12 Idler's Gardens

RIVER

N

1

Fight! Fight! Fight!

'SHOO!' SAID JOSHI, WAVING the insect away with his free hand. 'Buzz off!'

He didn't like bees. About a year ago, while taking cuttings from a rift orchid, one had stung him on the little finger and his hand had swelled to the size (and roughly the shape) of a Corrungian milking llama's udder. For three days he hadn't been able to hold a pruning knife, much less a garden fork or a spade.

Today Joshi wasn't taking any chances. He pulled his hooded brown cloak tightly around himself and darted between the flower stalls in the direction of Tinkers Alley.

He didn't get there.

'Not so fast!' a loud — and vaguely familiar — voice brayed in his ear.

Before Joshi realised what had happened, he was lying face down on the filthy cobblestones. A heavy boot rested on his buttocks, and a sword tip was pressed none too gently against the back of his neck.

'Thought you could sneak away did you, you lily-livered Blue?' sneered his burly assailant.

'I'm not a Blue,' Joshi whimpered, as a crowd of eager fight enthusiasts formed a circle around them. 'I'm a Green. It's me, Uncle Terrak — Joshi Nibhelline.'

Slowly the boot removed its pressure. With a flick of the sword blade, Joshi's hood was flipped to one side.

'Skyfire!' Terrak Nibhelline muttered angrily. 'I nearly ran you through, you useless pig's bladder! What in Mushin's name are you doing, masquerading as a Blue?'

'I'm not —' Joshi began, then let his voice trail away. Lying on the cobbles next to him, their broken stems still clutched in his grazed left hand, was a scatter of bedraggled blue flowers. A lone bee circled above them.

'It's not what you think, Uncle Terrak. They're

Tolrush poppies. Sera at the rose stall got them for me from a rift trader. I'm going to get the seeds and try to —'

'Enough!' roared Terrak, who wore a green cape over his dented armour and a chain of paper daisies — also dyed green — around his neck. 'You're a disgrace to the name of Nibhelline! Don't you know what day this is?'

Joshi swallowed. How could he *not* know? From the other side of the flower market came the battle cries of the Greens and the Blues, interspersed with the clashing of swords, as the two dominant families of Quentaris, the Nibhellines and the Duelphs, came head-to-head in what was *supposed* to be a harmless re-enactment of an ancient battle. But, as usual, things had got out of hand.

'It's Battle of the Begonias Day,' Joshi murmured.

'That's right,' said his uncle, savagely grinding the incriminating blue poppies into the cobbles with the heel of his right boot. 'It's the one day in the year when us Greens get a chance to show those gutter-crawling Blues what we're made of.'

'You're in luck then,' observed a deep, slightly out-of-breath voice. 'C'mon, show us what you're made of, Green weevil!'

Joshi, still lying on the cobbles, swivelled his

eyes sideways. And drew in his breath. The onlookers had parted, allowing a huge blue-clad warrior into the circle. He carried the biggest sword Joshi had ever seen and there was blood all along both its razor-sharp edges — Nibhelline blood, Joshi had no doubt.

'It's Hulk Duelph!' somebody said in an awed whisper.

Joshi knew him by reputation. Everybody did. Hulk Duelph was the Blues' master swordsman. Nobody in Quentaris could match him.

Clang! A sword landed on the cobbles just inches from Joshi's ear. One look at the Blue giant and Terrak Nibhelline had dropped his weapon and disappeared into the crowd like a cave rat fleeing from a stampede of rampaging Zolka.

'Boo! Bad form! Coward!' the fight enthusiasts called after him.

Hulk shook his head sadly and slid his own sword into its scabbard. Another Blue warrior had emerged from the wall of spectators behind him, a fierce-looking girl with curly red-bronze hair and a rapier held at the ready. Joshi guessed she was Hulk's sister, Taschia. According to rumour, her fighting skills were almost equal to her big brother's, and her temper was legendary. Confronted with these two, it was no wonder that Uncle Terrak had run away.

'It's your lucky day, cousin Blue,' said the girl, helping Joshi to his feet. 'If we hadn't come along when we did, that snivelling Green would have had your guts for greaves-liners.'

'He isn't a Blue,' one of the onlookers interjected.

Taschia looked questioningly at the fat, bearded peasant who had spoken and the man pointed an accusing finger in Joshi's direction.

'That fellow you supposedly rescued, Miss Duelph — he's a Green.'

Taschia frowned at Joshi, then at the crushed poppies lying at his feet. 'What's a Nibhelline doing with blue flowers?'

'I like flowers,' Joshi murmured sheepishly.

'Even *blue* ones?' asked the Blue swordsgirl.

Joshi shrugged. 'There's no such thing as a green flower. Anyway, I like all flowers. I grow them.'

'Pansy!' someone jeered.

Hulk scowled at the crowd. That shut them up. His sister fixed Joshi with an icy stare. 'Prove you aren't,' she challenged him.

'Prove I'm not what?' he asked nervously.

'A pansy.' She picked up Terrak's sword, twirled it on her thumb like a conjuror's whirlisnake, then offered it to him, pommel-first. 'Show us what you're made of, greenie.'

Joshi had no choice. Warily he accepted the sword. 'B-but … I'm not a fighter.'

'You're a Nibhelline, aren't you?' Taschia Duelph asked, carving a figure of eight in the air with her swishing rapier. 'It's Battle of the Begonias Day. C'mon, take a swing!'

'But … but … but,' stammered Joshi, his palm already sweaty on the sword's elk-horn grip. 'You'll make mincemeat of mc!'

The Blue girl laughed. 'That's the general idea. Tell you what, though — how about we even things up a bit?' She tossed her rapier deftly from one hand to the other. 'Look, to give you a more sporting chance, I'll fight with my left hand!'

Joshi swallowed. He should have run away when Terrak did. He turned to Hulk, standing at the edge of the crowd with his muscly arms folded and a wide grin on his face. 'I've never fought anyone in my life,' Joshi appealed to him, hoping he might call his sister off. 'I'm just a gardener.'

'A *gardener!*' The Blue giant raised his eyebrows. 'Haven't you got servants to do that?'

'It's kind of a hobby,' Joshi explained. 'Something I do because I enjoy it.'

'How can you *enjoy* gardening?' asked Taschia, lowering her rapier several inches.

Joshi felt a spark of hope. Both Duelphs were listening to him. Taking him seriously. Which was more than most members of *his* family ever did. 'I guess gardening for me,' he said, warming to the topic, 'is kind of like how sword fighting must be for you and your brother.'

It was a bad example. Taschia's eyes lost their thoughtful look. They became narrow and mean. She raised her rapier again. 'Quit stalling, greenie. On guard!'

Joshi swallowed nervously and raised his uncle's heavy sword. Its tip was visibly shaking.

'*Fight! Fight! Fight!*' yelled the circle of blood-crazed onlookers.

The two combatants circled each other. Taschia looked calm and focused, whereas Joshi's heart was beating faster than the wings of a hovering griffin. Don't panic, he counselled himself. If he panicked, he was liable to end up dead. His Blue opponent was a master of swordplay. But Joshi knew he might be able to match her if he kept his head and didn't let her reputation intimidate him. She was using her left hand, after all. And Joshi had a height advantage, as well as a longer reach. He was strong, too. Gardening — all that digging, all that pruning, all those heavy barrow loads of soil, animal dung and compost he'd wheeled up from the farmlands to the east of the city — had developed his muscles well beyond those of most fifteen-year-olds.

But a gardener's reflexes are no match for those of a trained fighter. Taschia's first thrust took Joshi completely off guard. Her rapier flashed under his sword arm with the speed of a striking viper.

Crunch!

She hit him dead centre, right in the chest. It would have been the end of him had Joshi not been wearing his cloak. The rapier's deadly point rebounded harmlessly off the garment's thick bronze clasp. But the force of it sent him staggering backwards.

'Oooooooo!' went the crowd.

Joshi regained his balance and made a wild swing in Taschia's direction. Dainty as a unicorn, she danced back out of his reach and his sword swished harmlessly through empty air.

'Aaaaaaah!' went the crowd.

The two combatants squared up to each other once more. This time Joshi was more wary. He watched the girl's eyes. When they narrowed slightly, he knew she was about to launch another attack. Summoning all his strength, he swung his sword sharply up and across. It was a tremendous gamble — Taschia hadn't even started moving yet. If Joshi had miscalculated, he would leave himself wide open to a counter attack. But just as he had guessed, the girl tried to repeat her previous move. This time steel met steel with a loud, bone-jarring *clang!*

When Taschia danced backwards, she was holding only half a rapier. Joshi's heavy sword had severed its thin blade ten inches from the hilt.

'*Wohhhhhh!*' went the crowd.

Taschia's face turned pink. 'Lucky blow,' she said, her eyes flashing in anger. She tossed her shortened rapier from her left hand to her right.

'Hey, that's not fair!' Joshi puffed. 'You said you'd fight with your left hand.'

'I'll tell you what isn't fair,' she snapped back at him. 'Fighting someone whose sword has been chopped in half isn't fair!'

'I didn't start this,' Joshi pointed out.

'Granted,' Taschia said, and gave him a mean little smile. '*I* started it. And now I'm going to finish it, greenie.'

This time Joshi was too slow to react. She was through his guard before he saw her coming. He heard a clash of steel, felt a jarring blow to his wrist, saw his sword falling from his numbed fingers. He found himself falling backwards.

By the time he regained his senses, Joshi was lying flat on his back on the cold cobblestones, with the sharp, broken point of Taschia's rapier pressed hard against his quivering throat.

'*Finish him! Finish him! Finish him!*' roared the crowd.

Joshi looked up into Taschia's grim, sweat-streaked face. And saw her eyes begin to narrow.

2

The
Bee Girl

THE BEE CAME OUT of nowhere. Alighting on Taschia's ear, it plunged its needle-sharp stinger deep into the soft pink flesh of her ear lobe.

To give the Blue swordsgirl credit, she didn't cry out. But she flinched, her eyes widened in pain and surprise. And for the space of a heartbeat, her rapier relaxed its pressure on Joshi's throat.

He seized the chance. Grabbing Taschia's wrist with both hands, Joshi forced her arm upwards.

'Oh no you don't!' she muttered, blinking away the pain of the bee sting.

Wrapping her left hand around her straining right wrist, Taschia pushed down on the weapon with all her strength. Its jagged silver tip wavered six inches above Joshi's exposed neck. He was supporting Taschia's full weight, including her heavy body-armour. Normally he would have been strong enough to push her clear, but his right arm had been numbed by Taschia's rapier blow and it wobbled like a badly set jelly. Slowly she forced the rapier down. The gap reduced to five inches. Four. Her face was red with effort, her eyes were narrowed to slits. Three inches.

'*Finish him!*' roared the bloodthirsty crowd.

Two inches. Joshi had no feeling in his right arm. He didn't know how much longer he could resist Taschia's determined onslaught. Her face hovered less than a foot above him. She was grimacing with effort, but even so the corners of her mouth twitched upwards in anticipation of victory.

One inch.

Joshi knew he was about to die. He felt faint. There was a strange buzzing sound in his ears. Black spots whirled in front of his eyes, darting back and forth between his face and Taschia's. He didn't want to look at her, didn't want to see that cruel, mocking grin. Didn't want to give her the satisfaction of seeing the fear in his eyes. So he clenched his eyes shut. Next moment, cold steel pressed against his windpipe. *This is it!* he thought.

Then he felt … nothing.

Was he dead?

Joshi opened his eyes. Inexplicably, the rapier was gone. So was Taschia. For several seconds he lay there, dazed, looking up at the black spots that continued to swirl and dart across the empty patch of blue sky where Taschia Duelph's head had been. Joshi's ears were still buzzing, but now he heard another sound, too. It was high-pitched and sounded like voices. Raised voices. Screaming voices. A chorus of screaming voices.

Joshi sat up and looked round in confusion. The fight enthusiasts no longer encircled him. They were running off in all directions, screaming and waving their arms above their heads in a very peculiar manner. Only two people remained, Taschia and Hulk Duelph. They seemed to be playing a game. The girl was shimmying around in little circles, jiggling her body and arms and legs about like a participant at one of the City Watch's popular Blue Lantern Barn Dances. Her brother was chasing after her, holding his cape out in front of him as if he were a matador and Taschia were a bull.

Only when he looked more closely did Joshi see the reason for the pair's strange behaviour. Taschia was surrounded by a cloud of bees. They swarmed all over her. They clung to her clothing, her armour, her legs, her hands and her face. There were even bees tangled in her hair. The whole swarm seemed to be attacking her.

Hulk chased his sister in circles, swiping at the bees with his cape. They were stinging him, too, but the Blue giant ignored them. At last he caught up with Taschia and threw his cape completely over her. Wrapping the bulky garment around his sister like a funeral shroud, he lifted her bundled form over his shoulder and charged off through the now deserted flower market, with a yellow mist of bees in hot pursuit.

Joshi climbed slowly to his feet. He could scarcely believe his good luck. The timely arrival of the bee swarm had saved his life. But he wasn't out of danger yet. All around him, the air hummed with angry, darting insects. Joshi stood very still.

'It's all right, they won't hurt you,' a soft, husky voice said behind him.

Joshi turned and saw a slight, yellow-haired girl approaching. She pushed a brightly painted barrow. In the barrow was a tall wooden beehive. Bees swarmed around her like yellow smoke.

'Were those your bees that chased everyone away?' Joshi asked.

She didn't answer. It was a silly question anyway. All the beehives in and around Quentaris belonged to this girl. Her name was Abelha, but most people called her the bee girl. Joshi had never been close to her before — he had never dared, because of the bees — and he was surprised to see how young she was. She looked about fourteen. Yellow pollen clung to every square inch of her skin, hair and clothing. Joshi frowned when he saw the tears that cut two wriggly tracks down her pollen-dusted cheeks.

'What's the matter?'

'They're going to die,' Abelha sniffed, setting her barrow down. She squatted on the cobblestones and began gently gathering the bees that littered the ground like fallen blossoms. Some spun in aimless circles on the cobbles, others didn't move. 'Aren't you going to help?' she asked, without looking up.

'But won't they sting?' Joshi said doubtfully.

'Bees can only sting once,' said the girl. She sniffed back a tear. 'After that, they die.'

Joshi knelt beside her and gingerly picked up a weakly struggling bee. As he placed it in his palm, he saw a gaping hole in the insect's abdomen where its stinger had been ripped out. 'Why do they sting, if it causes them to die?'

'Usually it's to protect their hive.'

Joshi glanced at the barrow. 'Those Blues weren't threatening your hive.'

'They were threatening you,' Abelha said.

'What's that got to do with your bees?'

'You're the person who grows so many of their favourite flowers.'

'Your bees were protecting *me*?' Joshi asked.

The bee girl nodded. 'They do what I tell them.'

She had made a pouch with the front of her yellow smock and half-filled it with dead and dying bees. With a nod of her head, she indicated that Joshi should put his bees in, too. He had only gathered five or six.

Abelha closed her eyes and began to hum. The noise came from somewhere deep inside her, as if her lungs were full of bees. It had a slow, lilting rhythm like a funeral march, yet it wasn't exactly a tune. Joshi thought it was the saddest sound he had ever heard.

'I'm sorry,' he whispered. 'I mean, I'm grateful, of course, but I'm sorry, too. For causing your bees to die.'

There were other things he wanted to say, but Joshi was unable to find the words. All he could do was kneel beside Abelha and watch, blinking back his own embarrassing tears, as the strange, pollen-dusted girl lifted her face to the sky. She kept humming, but louder now. Her eyes were still closed and the sun made tiny jewelled rainbows in their long wet lashes.

Now Joshi heard another sound. At first he thought it was the distant hoofbeats of galloping horses. But as it slowly grew louder, he realised he was mistaken. The sound became a dull roar that made the very air pulsate. Even though it was not yet noon, an eerie yellow twilight fell over the market square. Joshi looked up. An orange cloud had moved across the sun. As he watched — first in wonder, then in fear — the cloud wound itself into a tall yellow tornado that came spiralling slowly down towards him.

'Ghost bees!' he gasped.

Beside him, Abelha didn't even open her eyes. But she stopped humming long enough to say, 'You had better go, flower boy.'

Joshi didn't need to be told twice. Snatching up the crushed remains of his Tolrush poppies, he turned tail and ran.

3

A Disgrace to the Family Name

'YOU GOT BEATEN BY a *girl!*' jeered Vindon Nibhelline.

'It was Taschia Duelph,' Joshi said, loosening the soil around the roots of a rare Ulovatian dragon-lily he'd raised from a seedling in a secluded corner of the Idler's Gardens. 'Hulk's sister.'

'Do you know how old she is, Josephine?'

'My name's Joshi, not Josephine.'

'I think Josephine suits you better. Because no self-respecting *boy* — especially not a Nibhelline — would let himself get whipped by a thirteen-year-old girl!' Vindon crowed delightedly. '*And* she was fighting left-handed!'

Joshi didn't know how his cousin had found out. Like most bullies, Vindon had a big nose when it came to sniffing out gossip. Joshi stooped to pull up a weed.

'At least I didn't run away like your father did,' he muttered.

Vindon grabbed him by the neck of his tunic and pushed him face down into the freshly tilled soil. 'My father didn't run away, you snivelling piece of horse dung! He was giving Hulk Duelph a lesson in swordsmanship before that crazy bee girl came along and broke up the party.'

Joshi struggled for air. Vindon had a knee pressed painfully into his back and was twisting his collar from behind, nearly choking him. 'That's not what happened,' he gasped. 'As soon as Hulk and his sister showed up, your father —'

'Break it up, you two!' barked an authoritative female voice.

Strong hands pulled Vindon upright, then Joshi too was dragged roughly to his feet. A burly man in uniform held him in an iron-like grip. Another held Vindon, whose face had turned as red as one of Joshi's magnificent dragon-lilies behind them.

'Well, well, well,' said a tall, raven-haired woman with eyes like chips of emerald beneath black, lowered eyebrows. It was Commander Storm of the City Watch. 'As if yesterday's Green versus Blue debacle wasn't enough, now we have Green fighting Green!'

'Josephine here started it,' Vindon said.

'Silence!' snapped Commander Storm. She drummed her fingertips on the pommel of her sword and glared at Vindon. 'I know you, don't I? You're Terrak's boy. A born troublemaker, same as your father. But you,' she turned to Joshi. 'Frankly, I'm surprised and disappointed. You're the lad who looks after the gardens, the one Nibhelline in all of Quentaris who I thought had enough good sense to rise above all this Battle of the Begonias nonsense.'

'I wasn't actually —' Joshi began.

'Don't waste your breath making excuses. I heard all about your little set-to with Hulk Duelph and his sister.' The tall, black-clad woman arched her regal eyebrows. 'That took intestinal fortitude, I'll grant you, but it was also very stupid. You would have wound up as dead as an odod bird if Abelha hadn't come to your rescue.'

Joshi hung his head. It seemed that all of Quentaris had heard about yesterday's incident in the flower market. He was never going to live it down.

'I ought to lock both of you up for affray in a public place,' growled Commander Storm. 'But since my cells are already full to overflowing with other sorry survivors of yesterday's fiasco, I think I'll leave it to your family to deal with the pair of you.

'Take them to Drass,' she ordered her two burly officers.

Drass Nibhelline, patriarch of the Greens, was in a dark mood. Not only had he received a very painful blow on the nose from a flying pumpkin during yesterday's Battle of the Begonias celebrations, but today the city criers were declaring the re-enact-ment an overwhelming victory to the Blues. Obviously Lady Cyressa, Head of House Duelph, had offered them a greater bribe than he had.

And now he had been interrupted in the middle of lunch by two officers of the City Watch, with the disturbing report that the two young Greens stand-ing before him in his dining chamber had been fighting *each other!*

'What have you got to say for yourselves?' the red-faced Head of House Nibhelline demanded as soon as Commander Storm's men had gone.

'He started it,' Vindon said.

'I did not!' gasped Joshi. 'I was just minding my own business, then he came along and attacked me.'

'He called my father a coward,' said Vindon.

'He *is* a coward,' said Joshi.

'Why you snivelling piece of —'

'Enough!' roared Drass Nibhelline, leaning back in his chair and tiredly rubbing his two blackened eyes with the balls of his thumbs. 'You're giving me a headache. Now, I want you to tell me, slowly and *quietly,* what happened.'

Joshi and Vindon both started talking at once. 'I was just ...' 'He called my father ...'

'Stop!' cried Drass. 'Just one of you. Vindon, would you be so kind?'

And so Vindon gave his version of events — not a word of which was true. Joshi had to stand there, without uttering a word, until his cousin had finished.

'It wasn't like that at all!' he said finally.

Drass glared at him. 'Did I ask you to speak, boy? Frankly, it surprises me that you can stand here and look me in the eye. I heard what happened yesterday. How you got beaten by a ten-year-old girl.'

'Taschia's thirteen, sir,' Joshi said softly. 'And

she's a very skilled fighter. I had never even picked up a sword until yesterday.'

'I know all about you, Joshi,' said the Head of House Nibhelline and there was disappointment in his tone. 'You call yourself a Green, yet you'd rather hold a shovel than a sword.'

Joshi looked down his feet. He was aware of Vindon beside him, gloating at his discomfort. 'I don't see anything wrong with gardening, sir.'

'It's the work of commoners.' Drass shook his head and sighed. 'You're a Nibhelline. Where's your pride, boy?'

'I'm proud of what I do, sir,' Joshi said. He pointed at a vase of pretty, star-shaped leaves in a vase on the table near Drass's elbow. 'Where did you get those?'

The big, red-bearded man stared vaguely at the vase. 'How should I know? One of my servants probably put them there.'

'They would have found them growing up the north wall of the Archon's palace. It's Hallovian Ivy — there's only one plant of its kind in all of Quentaris. I bought the seed from a rift trader last year.'

'You would have been better to spend your

money on sword-fighting lessons,' quipped Vindon and Drass laughed appreciatively.

Joshi sighed. Yesterday he had seen at least a dozen Nibhelline warriors wearing Hallovian Ivy as decoration on their helmets. 'I make the city green,' he said. 'Because of me, even Lord Chalm's palace bears the colour of our family.'

Drass eyed the ivy suspiciously. 'What sort of flowers does it have?'

'They're only small,' said Joshi. 'But they're star-shaped, just like the leaves.'

'What colour are they?' Drass pressed.

Joshi moistened his lips. 'Blue,' he said softly.

'Blue!' roared the Head of House Nibhelline. With a sweep of one hairy hand, he knocked the vase over, sending it and the ivy crashing to the floor. 'Get out of my sight, boy! You're a disgrace to the family name!'

As Joshi hurried out of the room, he heard Vindon sniggering behind him. And a snippet of conversation.

'Have you had lunch, young Vindon?'

'Actually no, Uncle Drass.'

'Why don't you join me then? Cook's loshing-berry scones are especially good today.'

4

The Green
Petal

IT WASN'T FAIR, JOSHI brooded as he forked pig
manure into his handcart. Vindon was a sneak
and a liar, yet Drass had believed every word
he'd said. Furthermore, the Head of House
Nibhelline had even invited him to stay for lunch.
Whereas Joshi had been sent away in disgrace.
Why? Because Hallovian Ivy had blue flowers.

'Well, I don't care!' Joshi muttered aloud. 'All
flowers are good — it doesn't matter *what* colour
they are.'

'I couldn't agree with you more.'

Joshi got such a fright he nearly dropped his
wooden gardening fork. 'Abelha!' he gasped,
looking round in surprise.

'Sorry to startle you.' The bee girl smiled. 'I saw you working in here and thought I'd come and say hello.'

They were outside the city walls in a small, fenced allotment owned by Malodour, the pig farmer. Because of the pigs' snuffling and grunting, Joshi hadn't heard Abelha approach. She had left her barrow, with its buzzing beehive, just outside the gate. Only a small cloud of bees — a hundred or so — had accompanied her into the enclosure.

'You seemed upset about something,' she said.

Keeping a wary eye on the circling bees, Joshi told Abelha about his encounter with Drass Nibhelline. He shook his head sadly. 'Everyone laughs at me,' he sighed.

'I don't,' said the small, pollen-dusted girl standing barefoot among the smelly leavings of Malodour's pigs.

Joshi felt his face grow hot. 'But my family does. If you're a Nibhelline, you aren't supposed to get your hands dirty. Gardening is peasants' work.'

Abelha spread her own hands. 'Like keeping bees, I suppose.'

'It's different for you,' said Joshi. 'You aren't a Green or a Blue. And anyway, everyone loves your honey.'

'They love your gardens, too. If it wasn't for you, flower boy, Quentaris would be a grey and dreary place.'

Joshi shrugged. 'Sometimes I wonder if people notice.'

'*I* notice. And so do my bees,' said Abelha. She reached into the beaded hessian pouch slung round her neck. 'Here's a little thank you gift from them and me.'

It was a palm-sized section of honeycomb, wrapped in sticky brown parchment. Joshi opened one end and took a small bite.

'It's delicious,' he said, licking his lips. He noticed several of Malodour's pigs watching him hungrily, but he wasn't going to share the honey with them. 'Thank you, Abelha. And thank your bees for me, too.'

'You can thank them yourself, if you like,' she said mischievously.

Joshi glanced at her barrow with its swarming beehive just outside the gate. 'I'd rather not.'

'Scared of bees, are you, flower boy?' the girl teased.

'A little,' he admitted, nearly dropping the honeycomb when one landed on it. 'By the way, my name's Joshi.'

'That's a nice name. Sorry if I upset you by calling you flower boy.'

'It doesn't upset me. It's what I am, isn't it? Flower boy, the Nibhelline family disappointment.'

Abelha's face coloured slightly under its coating of pollen. 'I don't think you're a disappointment, Joshi,' she said. 'And I'm sure your parents don't, either.'

'Mum's quite understanding about it — or she pretends to be — but I know I embarrass my father. He used to be a professional second before Commander Storm made duelling illegal and he's always offering to give me sword-fighting lessons. But I wouldn't be any good at it — I don't have the killer instinct.' Joshi sighed and took another bite of honeycomb. 'I wish there was some way I could make them proud of me.'

'There's something on your lip,' Abelha said. She reached up and lightly brushed the corner of his mouth. 'Just a petal,' she said, showing him a little spear of greenery stuck to her fingertip with honey.

'You mean a leaf,' Joshi corrected her.

'No, it's a petal.'

'But that's impossible — it's green.'

'So?' said Abelha.

'There's no such thing as a green flower.'

Abelha shrugged. She carefully peeled the sticky piece of plant matter off her finger and dabbed it onto Joshi's palm. 'See for yourself.'

Joshi examined it closely. It *did* look like a petal. A green petal! Heart racing, he lightly touched the corner of his mouth. 'Where do you suppose it came from?' he asked.

'It must have been on the honeycomb,' Abelha said. 'Sorry.'

'But how did it get on the honeycomb?'

'From one of my bees. They often come back with those petals stuck to their legs and bodies. Sometimes they're even stuck to their wings!'

Joshi wasn't sure if he had heard her correctly. 'Your bees *often* come back with green petals on them?'

Abelha nodded. 'One or two every day. They're the stickiest of all petals — always covered in nectar. My bees love them.'

Joshi could barely contain his mounting excitement. Green petals meant green flowers. If he could find these flowers, harvest their seeds and grow them in time for next year's Battle of the Begonias Day, his family — even his extended family — would *have* to respect him. He'd be the toast of House Nibhelline!

'Do you know where the green flowers grow, Abelha?'

She shook her head. 'Only my bees know.'

It had to be somewhere beyond the Great River. He looked up at the cloud of insects that circled Abelha's head like a shimmering golden halo. 'If only bees could talk,' he said wistfully.

The bee girl gave him a puzzled half-smile. 'Of course bees can talk, Joshi!' she laughed. 'You just have to know their language.'

5

Deadly
Cave

THE LANGUAGE OF HONEY bees, Abelha explained, had more to do with signs and movement than it did with sound. When a bee found a field of fresh flowers, it returned to the hive and performed an intricate flower dance that told its fellow bees the exact location of its find. By turning in circles and waggling its body in a certain way, the bee let the others know which direction to take, and how far they would have to fly. It was a complicated language and even Abelha didn't fully understand it, but she did know that two right-hand circles, followed by three fast body-waggles, meant north.

'But it can't be north,' Joshi said to her. 'The Great River is south of us.'

It was shortly before noon two days after their conversation in Malodour's pig enclosure. They had spent almost every daylight hour of the intervening time patrolling Abelha's many beehives both in and around Quentaris, searching for bees with green petals stuck to them.

For Joshi it had been a frustrating time. When Abelha looked inside (Joshi always stood well back), she found green petals stuck to the honeycomb in almost all the hives, but none attached to bees. Until now. The bee girl was crouched over a hive behind the stables at the Old Tree Guesthouse, and a worker bee with a green petal stuck to its wing was performing a flower dance for a crowd of her excited sister-bees at the hive's entryway.

'She definitely says north,' Abelha said.

Already several bees were flying off in that direction.

'But there's nothing to the north ...' Joshi said, watching them go. His eyes slowly shifted upwards from the ribbon of departing bees and focused on the wall of forbidding, mist-capped granite peaks that towered over the city.

Except the rifts! he thought with a shiver.

'Are you going to stand there dreaming all day?' asked the bee girl. 'Or are you going to help me?'

He snapped out of his trance. Abelha was walking back to her barrow. She had left it and its buzzing cargo under the massive oak tree, after which the guesthouse was named.

'Help me lift this off,' she said, leaning over the hive in her barrow.

'Wh-why?' stammered Joshi, keeping well back.

'Because the bees in *this* hive don't know the way to your precious green flowers. It's the bees in *that* hive,' she pointed at the one near the stables, 'that are going to lead us there. Come on, give me a hand.'

'W-won't they sting me?'

'Not if you hum to them.'

'I thought you said bees talk by dancing, not sound,' Joshi said as he nervously approached the slight, barefoot girl in her protective mist of bees.

'That's when they talk to *each other*,' said Abelha. She grinned impishly. 'But you can dance if you like, flower boy.'

Joshi hummed loudly as he helped Abelha lift the buzzing hive from her barrow. She hummed too, but more quietly (and more tunefully) and Joshi sensed that it was her soothing notes rather than his that calmed the swarming insects. Even though it was impossible to lift the wooden hive without squashing two or three bees, not a single one stung him. He and Abelha left the hive under the old oak tree, then replaced it with the one near the stables.

'Now my darlings,' the bee girl said to her bees as she lifted her barrow and turned it towards the courtyard gate, 'lead us to the green flowers.'

It was Imbleday noon and the city streets were choked with shoppers, merchants, hawkers, street urchins, loiterers, pickpockets, soldiers, adventurers, goblins, elves, bog sylphs, shifty-eyed trolls and many other exotic-looking rift travellers of races unknown to Joshi. The milling throngs were so thick that it should have taken the better part of an hour to travel any distance at all. But the crowds parted ahead of Abelha's bee swarm as if by magic, giving them a free and uninterrupted journey all the way to the Last and First Station.

One look at Abelha and her travelling beehive, and the two guards at the main gate waved them through without even demanding a toll. Associating with the bee girl, Joshi realised, had its compensations.

'Watch out for Zolka, Miss Abelha,' warned one of the guards, quickly lowering his helmet visor as a curious bee circled its pink, flamingo-feather plume. 'An adventurer who came through the Kladonica Rift this morning reported seeing fresh tracks.'

'Thanks for the warning,' she said. 'We'll keep well away from there.'

'Do you need a rift map?' the other guard asked. 'I can let you have a slightly used one for two copper rounds.'

'Thank you, but we can find our own way,' Abelha declined politely.

Joshi waited until the massive wood and iron gates had clanked closed behind them before he spoke. 'You don't seriously intend to go into the rift caves?' he asked in a low voice.

'It depends where my bees lead us,' said Abelha. She stopped and set her barrow down. Her pollen-dusted forehead creased in a frown. 'Speaking of which, did you see which way they went?'

They both searched the sky. Bees buzzed and flitted and circled all around them, but it had been some time since they had seen any flying off to the north.

'Maybe they've lost their way,' suggested Joshi.

The bee girl made a snorting sound. 'Bees don't get lost! Only humans get lost. Look, here comes one now.'

She had the eyes of a hawk. Joshi didn't see the insect for several more seconds. Then it came zipping out of the shadow of the towering cliffs like a small yellow and green dart moth. The flecks of green on the approaching bee set Joshi's heart fluttering. There was not one, but *three* green petals plastered to its legs and furry body. The new arrival landed on the front of the barrow, where it was immediately surrounded by a crowd of its sisters from the hive. It began to dance. Two right-hand circles, followed by three fast body-waggles.

'North!' Abelha said, sounding pleased with herself.

The other bees began taking off and heading in that direction. Quick as a praying mantis, Abelha plucked one out of the air and held it between her thumb and forefinger. Joshi felt sure it would sting her, but the insect didn't even struggle. Humming to her captive, the bee girl bit through the hem of one of her long silken sleeves. Capturing a loose thread with her free hand, she quickly unravelled it, drawing out the spiderweb-thin cotton thread until it was nearly a yard in length. Then she snipped it off with her teeth.

'Hold your hand flat,' she said to Joshi.

He nervously did as she asked. Still humming softly, Abelha placed the captive bee gently on his palm. The insect seemed to be in a trance. It sat there without moving as the bee girl deftly tied one end of the cotton thread around its middle. Then she bent her head and whispered to it, 'Fly!' The bee immediately took to the air. But it didn't get far — only a yard — before the cotton twanged taut and the bee whirled at the end of its leash like a tiny, living kite.

'Bring the barrow, Joshi,' Abelha said over her shoulder. She went running off ahead, with the tethered bee buzzing and spiralling in front of her.

Joshi followed as fast as he dared, but the path was steep and bumpy as it wound its way up into the cliffs, and Abelha was soon out of sight. Joshi found himself alone with a barrow-load of bees. It wasn't a good feeling. Each time the barrow's small wooden wheel went over a rock or a bump or a protruding root, bees poured out of the hive and buzzed threateningly around his head. *Help!* Joshi thought, breaking into a nervous sweat. Soon the cloud of swirling, angry-sounding insects became so thick that he could barely see where he was going.

He considered leaving the barrow at the side of the track, but Abelha had asked him to bring it and he didn't want her to think him a coward. Besides, she was doing him a favour by helping him look for the green flowers.

But what good would green flowers be, Joshi asked himself, to someone who'd been stung to death by bees?

At least he'd be the first Nibhelline to have green flowers on his grave!

That thought failed to cheer him up, however. 'Abelha!' he called.

But he got no answer.

Even if she did answer, Joshi realised, he would never hear her above the swarm's loud buzzing.

A bee landed on his nose and he looked at it, cross-eyed. Gently, Joshi set the barrow down. 'Shoo!' he said, waving his hands in front of his face.

The bee stayed where it was. It buzzed. That gave Joshi an idea. Puckering his lips, he began to hum softly. The bee stopped buzzing for a moment, then flickered its wings and rose into the air. Joshi hummed louder. As it had done back at the Old Tree Guesthouse, the sound calmed the swarming bees and most of them flew back into the hive. Those that didn't, went flying off in search of flowers. Green flowers, Joshi hoped. Soon he was able to lift the barrow again and continue up the steep narrow path, humming loudly with every step.

There was still no sign of Abelha. Where had she gone? Joshi hated being left alone with her barrow-load of bees. Moreover, he hated being here, high above the city, up near the famous Quentaran rift caves, without an escort or a guide. With only his pruning knife to protect himself. Not that a pruning knife would be much use, he supposed, against a Zolka, or any of the other blood-sucking, bone-crunching, marrow-eating monstrosities that were liable to come swarming out of the caves at any moment.

He was among the caves now. The first one he passed had a wooden sign out the front. Elven Cave. That didn't sound so bad — Joshi liked elves. No other race could grow sunflowers two feet across. Or buttercups as *big* as cups.

The next opening was marked Deadly Cave. It was shaped like the gaping mouth of an asp, with two long, yellowed stalactites that resembled fangs. A shiver ran up and down Joshi's spine and he nearly stopped humming. He pushed the bee girl's barrow as quickly as he dared past its forbidding black maw.

'Stop right where you are, Quentaran!' a loud, unearthly voice came echoing out of the darkness.

6

I Hope the Zolka Get You!

JOSHI NEARLY DROPPED THE barrow. 'Abelha?' he gasped, his heart jumping like a frog in a box of tickler worms as he peered into the cave.

'How did you know it was me?' she asked, her voice still echoey, but more recognisable now that she wasn't shouting.

Joshi strained his eyes into the gloom. He could see her shadowy form about ten yards in from the entrance. 'What are you doing in there?'

'It's where the bees are going,' Abelha said. 'Come and have a look.'

Joshi left the barrow outside the cave mouth and

tiptoed in to join the bee girl. She was standing at the side of the cave — with one arm buried all the way to the shoulder in its rocky wall!

'Abelha, what happened?' Joshi asked, staring at her arm in shock. 'Was there a rock fall?'

She shook her head. 'Look!' she said, and pulled her arm free. It slid out of the rock as easily and smoothly as an oar coming out of water.

'H-how did you do that?' whispered Joshi.

Abelha smiled mysteriously. She held a fine cotton thread in her fingers. Its other end disappeared into the rock wall where her arm had been. Even in the poor light, Joshi could see the thread moving, as if something was alive inside the rock, jiggling it back and forth.

'Is it ... a rift?' he asked.

She nodded. Joshi's eyes were adjusting to the semi-darkness and for the first time he noticed a faint glow in the rock where the cotton disappeared. Abelha pulled on the cotton and out came a bee.

'Here's where they're going to get your green flowers,' she said.

The moment she spoke, another bee came buzzing into the cave from the barrow outside. It spent a few moments circling the faintly glowing section of rock, then flew directly at it and was swallowed by the cave wall.

'Try it, Joshi,' Abelha said.

Tentatively, he extended his hand. There was a faint tingling sensation and a rash of goose bumps shot up his arm as first his fingertips, then his hand and his wrist disappeared from view.

'Well, if it isn't Quentaris's two most talked-about lovebirds!' someone said from outside the cave.

Joshi jerked his hand free. His face felt hot. *Lovebirds.* 'Vindon, what are you doing here?'

'I could ask you the same question, Josephine,' Vindon smirked, swaggering in from the ring of bright daylight outside. He had his sword drawn. 'Don't you know it's dangerous, fooling around in the rifts without a guide?'

Joshi's face grew even hotter. 'Nobody's going into any rifts,' he said, stepping quickly in front of the faintly glowing section of rock.

Vindon extended his sword and firmly nudged Joshi aside with the flat of its blade; then he pushed the sword into the cave wall. Green sparks flashed along the tempered-steel blade as it passed soundlessly through the rock. 'By all that's holy!' he exclaimed. 'I didn't know there was one here! The main rift — the one leading to Borka — is farther into the cave. Every rift traveller and his dog must have walked right past this one without even knowing it existed!'

Vindon stepped back when two bees came buzzing out of the rock. He watched them fly off to the barrow, then turned to Abelha. When he saw the bee twirling at the end of its cotton leash, his eyes narrowed.

'What exactly are you two up to?'

'Nothing,' Joshi said.

Vindon clucked his tongue. 'Tut, tut, cuz, don't lie to me,' he said in a mocking voice. 'I've been following you and your girlfriend for the past two days. Thick as thieves, you are. I know you're up to something.'

'Mind your own business.'

'But this is my business, don't you see? You're my cousin, Joshi Nibhelline, and we Greens don't keep secrets from each other.'

'Well, *I'm* not a Green,' Abelha said softly, 'and what's my business definitely isn't yours, Vindon.'

'So you *can* talk, honey bee!' crowed Vindon. 'I was beginning to think you could only buzz like your little friends in the barrow outside.'

'I'll sic them on you, if you don't leave us alone,' she warned.

'Woo, touchy, touchy!' laughed Vindon. He sighed and shook his head. 'I don't know why you're both being so unfriendly. I only came along to offer my services.'

'We don't need your services,' Joshi said.

Vindon poked his sword into the rock again. 'Seems to me you do. Either of you been through a rift before? They can lead to some pretty dangerous places. And this is a new one — unexplored. Anything could be in there. You'll need a guide, someone to watch your back if things get sticky.'

'You aren't a guide,' Joshi said.

'True,' said Vindon. 'But I've been through one or two rifts in my time. And I can use a sword, which is more than I can say for you, Josephine.'

'Is there something wrong with your hearing?' Abelha asked. 'We don't *want* your help, Vindon. Go away and bother someone else!'

She waved one hand in the air and immediately Vindon was surrounded by a buzzing swarm of bees. They drove him towards the mouth of the cave.

'I hope the Zolka get you!' he called over his shoulder, then stomped out into the sunshine.

'He's a charming fellow, your cousin,' Abelha said when they were alone again.

Joshi watched another bee fly into the rock wall. 'Maybe he has a point, Abelha. We don't know what's on the other side of the rift.'

Her honey-brown eyes flashed him a look that was half-teasing, half-challenging. 'One way to find out,' she said.

And stepped boldly into the rock.

7

The
Monster

ALL HIS LIFE JOSHI had heard stories about the rifts. And many of them were horror stories. About people who returned injured or disfigured, or changed in some strange and frightening way. Only last sevenday a young adventurer had come back, after only three days away, with his hair turned as white as chalk. When asked what had happened, he had barked like a jackal. The sevenday before that, a Hadran fortune hunter had returned with leopard spots covering every square inch of his skin.

But the worst — and most common — stories concerned those who *didn't* come back. Many travellers simply became lost and couldn't find their way home through the labyrinthine caves. Or they couldn't find the rift they had come through. Some rifts opened and closed without warning, while others seemed to move from one place to another. So even with a map or a guide, rift travel could be a hazardous business.

And the hazards weren't confined to the danger of losing your way. As well as the Zolka — terrifying, beetle-like creatures as large as elephants — the rift caves were stalked by all manner of fearsome animals, reptiles, dragons, gargoyles, robbers, assassins and slave traders. And that was to say nothing of the hazards that lurked *beyond* the caves, in the strange and often dangerous lands a traveller entered by stepping through any of the rift portals.

Now that he was alone, Joshi found himself wishing more than ever that he hadn't sent his cousin away. Annoying as Vindon was, he did have some experience as a rift traveller. And he could use a sword. But now it was too late. Vindon was probably halfway back to the city gates. And Abelha had gone through the rift. Joshi had no alternative but to follow her.

'May the gods protect me,' he muttered, and pushed himself through the cave wall.

Or tried to. He only got halfway, then suddenly lost his nerve. And froze. All Joshi could see was half his body and one leg and one arm protruding from the mossy granite like a partially carved statue. The parts of him that were inside the rock felt tingly and numb. The exposed parts were stippled with goose bumps.

'Help!' he cried, and tried dragging himself out.

But something was gripping his other wrist — the one inside the rock — and pulling him the other way. For a moment Joshi panicked and fought against whatever it was. Then he came to his senses and realised it was Abelha. She was on the other side and so were the green flowers. The flowers they had been searching for the past two and a half days. The flowers that were going to change his life. Joshi took a deep breath and stopped resisting.

For a few frightening moments he was inside the rock. But it wasn't dark, as he'd expected. Instead, he found himself surrounded by an eerie green light. It was like being under water, except it wasn't cold and all around him were sparkling green stars that fizzed and popped against his skin and made his hair stand on end.

Then he was through the rift and now it *was*

dark. He was back in a cave, but something told him it wasn't the same cave he'd been in moments before. There was a shadowy form in front of him and a small hand clutched his.

'Abelha?' he said nervously.

'Ssssssh!' she warned, tightening her grip around his fingers. Her palm felt sweaty. 'There's something here.'

Joshi's skin crawled. 'You don't mean something ... *alive?*'

He sensed rather than saw Abelha nodding. The cave they were in was darker than Deadly Cave, but there was a pale wash of light in the distance, suggesting that the cave's mouth was not too far away. 'Where is it? I can't see anything.'

'Neither can I,' whispered Abelha. 'But you can hear it breathing. I think it's asleep. Listen.'

Joshi tried to listen, but at first all he could hear was his racing heart and the occasional bee that went buzzing past his head in the darkness. When he held his breath and concentrated, he heard another sound — a deep, rhythmic wheeze. It sounded like the rumble of distant thunder. Whatever was producing it must have been huge.

'Let's go back,' he hissed, tugging on Abelha's hand. 'It might be a Zolka, or even a dragon.'

She held her ground. 'Zolka and dragons don't eat honey.'

'How do you know it eats honey?'

'I can smell its breath.'

Joshi sniffed the air, but all he smelled was a musky, wild-animal odour that took him back to his childhood; back to the day his father had taken him to visit a travelling circus. *Holy Mushin!* Joshi suddenly thought. 'I think it's a *bear!*'

'There aren't bears in Quentaris,' Abelha whispered.

'We aren't *in* Quentaris,' he reminded her. He increased the pressure on her hand. 'C'mon, let's go back.'

'Don't you want to get some green flowers?'

'Not if it means being eaten by a bear.'

'I don't think they eat people,' Abelha whispered. 'Anyway, it's asleep. Let's sneak past and see what's outside.'

Once again Joshi found himself wishing that his cousin was with them. Vindon might have talked some sense into her. But somehow Joshi doubted it. Abelha was stubborn. Stubborn enough, he was beginning to think, to get them both killed. Now that they had been in the cave for some time, Joshi's eyes were beginning to adjust to the darkness and he could see the outline of the sleeping creature. Much too big to be a bear, it was a huge shapeless mound that almost completely blocked the cave ahead of them. Some sort of monster, he thought. Did Zolka have fur?

'There's no way past it,' he whispered, glad to have an excuse to turn back.

'There is,' said Abelha, 'if we climb onto that ledge.'

Joshi's heart sank. The ledge was about four feet off the ground and no more than eight inches across at its widest point. 'It's not big enough.'

'I'll hold your hand,' Abelha teased.

Already she was scrambling up onto the narrow ledge, her knees dislodging a clatter of debris that Joshi thought must surely awaken whatever it was sharing the cave with them. But the monster didn't move; its slow, steady breathing continued unabated. Joshi waited until Abelha was safely on the ledge, then climbed up after her. *What has she got us into?* he wondered as he struggled, slowly and shakily, upright. The ledge was too narrow to crawl along and there was barely room to stand. Above it, the cave wall began curving inwards towards the ceiling, forcing Joshi, who was taller than Abelha, to lean forward almost beyond the point of balance. One slip and he'd be monster food.

Pressing their backs to the cool, mossy wall, Joshi and Abelha began inching their way along the ledge past the mountainous black bulk of the sleeping creature. Even though they were four feet above the cave floor, they were still looking up at it.

If I ever make it back home, Joshi thought, *I'm never leaving Quentaris again. I'm a gardener, not an adventurer. It doesn't matter if people tease me.*

'Hey Josephiiiiiiiine!' a loud and all-too-familiar voice echoed around the cave. 'Where aaaaa-are yoooooou?'

There was a scuffling noise from the direction they had come, followed by the loud *rasp, rasp, rasp* of a flint striking rock.

'No, Vindon! *Don't!*' Joshi hissed, but he was too late.

All at once the cave was bathed in guttering yellow light. And there, at the mouth of the rift, with a smoky torch above his head and a silly grin on his face, stood Vindon.

8

Sword-for-hire

VINDON MUST HAVE FETCHED the torch in the belief that its smoke would protect him from Abelha's bees. But his triumphant grin changed slowly to a grimace of horror when he saw what was in front of him.

He'd woken the sleeping monster.

With a long, deep growl that rumbled like an avalanche, the creature raised its massive head. Joshi saw that it *was* a bear after all. But this was nothing like a circus bear. It was huge. Its head alone was the size of the bear Joshi had seen as a boy. Its body was as large as a house. When it raised itself onto its four shaggy, tree-trunk legs, its back brushed against the ceiling and it seemed to fill the whole cave. Joshi and Abelha flattened themselves against the wall as the bear's warm furry hide pressed against them. It didn't know they were there. Its attention was focused on Vindon. There was just room to see past its flank as the massive animal swayed slowly towards him.

Vindon was frozen in terror. He was so shocked that he hadn't even drawn his sword.

'Go *back!*' Joshi cried, even though he knew that to call out would alert the monster to his and Abelha's presence. 'Go back through the rift!'

A flicker of something that might have been understanding crossed Vindon's face. But he was too frightened to move. The flaming torch dropped from his fingers and he screamed. The sound seemed to weaken the bear's resolve. It stopped just short of him, lowered its massive head and regarded the torch. Obviously it had never encountered anything like it before, because it leaned cautiously forward and sniffed the flame, inadvertently sucking two yellow tongues of fire up into its nostrils.

All hell broke loose. The bear let out a howl so loud it brought a shower of dust and debris raining down from the ceiling. The howl turned to a thunderous roar of pain and rage as the huge animal backed away from the flickering flame, squeezed itself around in a half-circle and went lumbering off towards the cave entrance. As it brushed past Joshi and Abelha, its enormous shaggy body swept both of them off the ledge. But it wasn't far to fall and the cave floor was surprisingly soft. Neither of them were hurt.

'Poor bear,' Abelha said, picking herself up off the ground and wiping the dirt off her clothes.

'Poor *bear*?' gasped Joshi. 'It nearly killed us! And it would have eaten Vindon if it hadn't burned itself.'

'Well, that would hardly be a great loss to humanity,' she quipped.

'I heard that,' said Vindon, swaggering towards them with the flaming torch in one hand, his sword in the other. 'Hardly the thanks I expected, after saving both your sorry lives.'

Joshi laughed. 'It's a bit late to play the hero, Vindon. That's quite a scream you've got. Ever thought of joining a choir?'

'Don't get smart, Josephine!' Vindon warned.

'I wouldn't be calling people names if I were you, Vindon,' said Abelha. 'At least not till I'd changed my breeches.'

He glanced down at himself and his face turned red in the torchlight. There was a large wet stain on the front of his trousers. Sheathing his sword, he quickly untucked his tunic to cover it. 'Must be from when I squeezed through the rift,' he mumbled sheepishly. 'Those rocks were a bit damp.'

Looking at Vindon's untucked tunic, his wet trousers and his visibly trembling hands, Joshi almost felt sorry for him. Almost. 'Where did you get the torch, Vindon?'

'From a trader coming back from one of the caves farther up. I had to pay twenty rounds for it. I'll add it to my fee.'

'Your *fee?*' Joshi and Abelha both said together.

'For being your guide.'

'We don't *want* a guide!' Abelha cried in frustration. 'Haven't we made that clear?'

'But you'll need a sword-for-hire,' said Vindon. He motioned towards the distant glow of light that marked the cave entrance. 'Who knows what other nasties are lurking out there.'

Joshi had to admire his cousin's powers of recovery. Two minutes ago he'd been scared out of his wits, now he was back to his loud-mouthed worst. And Vindon did have a point. They might need someone to watch their backs. But could they trust him?

'All right, you can come along,' Joshi said,

wondering if he was making the right decision. 'But we're not paying you anything.'

Vindon nodded slowly. 'Very well. But I want a half share if we find any gold or treasure.'

Joshi hadn't even considered that they might find treasure. All he wanted was the green flowers. 'You can have a third share,' he decided, 'because there are three of us. But only if it's gold or treasure. If we find anything else, it's up to Abelha and me to decide what to do with it.'

'What else are you hoping to find?' his cousin asked suspiciously.

'That's our business. Do you agree to my conditions?'

Vindon hesitated. His eyes glinted craftily in the torchlight. 'I don't actually have to agree to anything, Josephine,' he said. 'I can come along with you two lovebirds, whether you like it or not. There's no way you can stop me.'

Abelha had stood silently in the shadows while the cousins negotiated. Now she began softly humming. Within a few moments, the cave echoed with an angry buzzing sound.

'Ever been stung by a bee, Vindon?' she asked innocently.

He waved the torch in frantic circles above his

head, but the flame and smoke did little to deter the swarming insects.

'Call them off!' he cried. 'I agree to your conditions.'

Abelha hummed again and the bees flew off into the surrounding darkness. 'Well, that's settled then,' she said brightly. She smiled at Vindon. 'What are you waiting for, sword-for-hire? Lead the way.'

9

World
of Giants

'LOOK AT THE SIZE of them!' gasped Joshi.

He, Abelha and Vindon stood at the cave entrance with their heads tipped right back. Their mouths hung open in amazement. They were standing in a forest, but this wasn't a normal forest — the trees were giants. Each enormous, greenish-brown trunk was as broad as a castle keep and taller than the eye could see. They went into the clouds!

'What is this place?' Abelha whispered.

Beside her, Vindon still held the flaming torch aloft, as if he had forgotten they were no longer in the cave. 'Don't ask me; I've never heard tell of it.

Maybe we're the first people to come here. These trees are unbelievable!'

'They must be a mile high!' said Joshi.

'The Frostopians are always looking for firewood,' his cousin said, a scheming look in his eyes. 'They pay in gold. We could sell them the timber rights to this place — we'd be rich!'

Joshi was shocked. 'These trees must be thousands of years old. You can't chop them down!'

'The Frostopians could. They've got axes made of iron so hard they can chop through rock.'

'Well, they're not getting these trees,' Joshi said firmly.

'Why not?' demanded Vindon. 'We could make a fortune, cuz.'

'Has it occurred to you,' Abelha asked, 'that these trees aren't ours to sell, Vindon?'

He laughed and turned in a circle. 'Look around you. Do you see anyone else here? Do you see any *sign* of anyone else? I reckon we're the first people to set foot in this place. I reckon anything we find is ours. We can split it three ways. We'll be set up for life!'

'Nobody's splitting up anything, Vindon,' Joshi muttered. 'Remember our agreement? Abelha and I get to decide.'

His cousin gave him a murderous look. 'You tricked me into making that agreement. I didn't know what was here.'

'Neither did we,' Joshi told him. 'And remember who found the rift in the first place.'

'My bees did,' Abelha said, surprising them both. She looked at Vindon, then at Joshi. 'Let's not waste our time arguing. For all we know, there might be a village in the next clearing. Let's take a look around first, then decide what to do.'

Joshi shivered. He had just noticed a massive paw print in the muddy earth at their feet — it was the size of a cart. 'I wonder where that bear went,' he said softly. Giant bears, giant trees — had they stumbled into a world of giants? 'Maybe we should just … go back.'

'You can go back if you like, Josephine,' Vindon said in a mocking tone. 'But if you do, our agreement no longer stands. Anything I find, I get to keep.'

Joshi glanced at Abelha. 'What do you think we should do?'

'It's up to you, Joshi,' she said. 'It was you who wanted to come here.'

He took a deep breath and turned back to

Vindon. 'I guess it would be pretty silly to go back without having a look around first.'

'Whatever you say, Josephine.'

Joshi gritted his teeth. 'Call me Josephine one more time,' he warned, 'and I'll punch you in the nose.'

Vindon let out a hoot of laughter. 'Listen to garden boy talking like a big strong man!' he chortled. Sticking the torch handle-first into the ground, he squared up to Joshi in a pugilist's stance. 'Give me your best shot, *Josephine!*'

Joshi raised his fists.

'Stop it, you two!' snapped Abelha, stepping quickly between them. 'If you're going to behave like a pair of ... Greens and Blues, then I'm going back to Quentaris.'

'Off you go then, honey bee,' Vindon said through his teeth.

'No, stay,' said Joshi, taking a step back. 'We won't fight.'

'Coward,' hissed Vindon. 'Hiding behind your girlfriend's skirts.'

'Why you ... !'

'*Stop it!*' shrieked Abelha. She waved her hands at the giant trees surrounding them. 'We know *nothing* about this place! There could be anything out there. If we want to survive, we'll need to watch out for each other, not tear each other to shreds!'

'I was only going to punch him in the nose,' Joshi said.

Vindon thrust his chin out. 'I'd like to see you try.'

'Boys! I said stop it!' Abelha warned. 'Now shake hands.'

Joshi folded his arms. 'Only if he apologises for calling me names.'

'Never!' Vindon said, folding his own arms.

Abelha folded her arms, too. And started humming. Within moments, the three of them were surrounded by bees.

'Shake hands,' Abelha said.

The two cousins shook hands. Reluctantly. There was a bit of finger squeezing and crunching of knuckles.

'That's enough,' said the bee girl. When they had both let go, she gave each of them a big smile. 'Now, will you both promise not to fight while I go back for my bees?'

Vindon scowled and waved a hand in the air. 'They seem to be here already, honey bee. In case you hadn't noticed.'

'Only the scouts and the nectar-seekers are here,' Abelha said pleasantly. 'I need to get the others.'

'Your barrow won't fit through the rift,' Joshi told her.

'I'll leave it and the hive on the other side.' She fingered the beaded pouch hanging round her neck. 'I'll just bring the bees.'

'Why didn't you bring them in the first place?' Joshi asked.

'I didn't know what it would be like on this side. A beekeeper never puts her colony in danger,' Abelha explained. 'Wait here, I won't be long.'

With that, she picked up the flaming torch and disappeared back into the cave. Only it wasn't a cave, Joshi saw now. It was a hollow log — an enormous hollow log. The cavernous, moss-lined, perfectly circular opening rose ten or twelve yards above their heads like a gateway to another world. Which, in effect, it was.

'Are there any other rifts that come out through fallen trees?' Joshi asked his cousin.

He was only trying to make conversation. A tense and awkward silence had fallen since Abelha had left the two of them on their own. But instead of answering, Vindon gave him a cold, squinty-eyed look.

Then, with no further warning, he dragged his sword from its scabbard and rushed straight at Joshi, swinging the deadly blade in a wide, hissing arc.

10

The
Hectapus

THERE WASN'T TIME TO react. There was barely time to think, other than to register the absolute injustice of what was about to happen. Joshi had always known Vindon wasn't to be trusted, but he hadn't realised — could never have imagined! — that his cousin was so cowardly, so downright *evil*, that he could cut down an unarmed opponent in cold blood. And all for what? Because Joshi had threatened to punch him in the nose!

'I didn't —' cried Joshi, but those were the only two words he uttered before Vindon's elbow struck him a numbing blow in the solar plexus, knocking all the wind out of him and toppling him sideways.

As he fell, Joshi glimpsed the silver sword blade flashing down, and knew he was about to die.

Crunch!

He heard, rather than felt, the blow. Then there was another and another — a whole series of blows, *crunchcrunchcrunchcrunch!* — yet Joshi felt nothing, other than the throbbing ache in his solar plexus where Vindon's elbow had struck him.

He realised he was rolling along the ground. Away from Vindon and away from the slashing sword. The sound of the blows continued — *crunchcrunchcrunch* — but it grew quieter as Joshi rolled away from it.

Why wasn't Vindon coming after him? And why, if he wasn't coming after him, was Vindon still hacking at the ground where Joshi had first fallen?

Joshi stopped rolling, but only because he had rolled all the way to one of the trees and bumped against it. The tree trunk was huge, like a section of a city wall. Breathing hard, still terrified that Vindon was pursuing him, Joshi raised his head and looked back. His cousin was twenty yards away, holding up a piece of knotted rope. And grinning.

'One more second and it would have got you,' he said.

The rope was twitching, Joshi noticed. Drops of purple liquid dribbled from it. Vindon raised his sword and sliced it in half. 'Nasty piece of work!' he said, throwing the thing away, then wiping his hand on his trouser leg.

Joshi struggled to his feet. It was painful to breathe. Vindon had hit him hard. He limped towards his cousin. The ground was littered with long ropey fragments, similar to the one Vindon had chopped in half. Obviously part of some ghastly, now-dead creature — either its legs or its arms — they were rusty bronze in colour and covered in slimy scales. What had looked like knots from a distance, now resembled a series of raised, circular mouths. Some of them still moved, making wet kissing sounds as they opened and closed. At the centre of the carnage, next to Vindon's boots, lay something that resembled a giant pumpkin, surrounded by a pool of oily purple liquid. But pumpkins aren't scaly and they don't have eyes. Nor do they have teeth.

'What was it?' Joshi asked, a shiver of revulsion passing through him.

'Dunno,' said Vindon. 'Looked a bit like one of those hectapuses the fishermen sometimes drag up from the Great River, only normal hectapuses aren't this big and they don't have scales. It was creeping up behind you. Would have got you, too, if I hadn't got it first.'

He saved my life, Joshi realised. 'Thanks, Vindon. I appreciate it.'

His cousin wiped his sword clean on some ferns, then slid the weapon back into its scabbard. 'Yeah, well; I figured if your girlfriend came back and found you dead, she might think I was to blame.'

'She isn't actually my girlfriend,' said Joshi.

'Whatever you say, cousin.' Vindon gave him a sly look. 'But I know you two are up to something. You didn't come here looking for treasure or gold, so what *are* you and honey bee after?'

'It's nothing that would interest you.'

'Why don't you let me be the judge of that, cousin? You owe me, after all.'

'What does he owe you?' asked a muffled voice behind them.

They both turned and saw a strange figure emerge from the mouth of the hollow log. Vaguely human in shape, it was covered from head to foot in a living chainmail of bees. In one hand it carried a small piece of honeycomb, in the other a smoking torch.

'Abelha?' gasped Joshi. Her eyes and nose were

visible through a tiny gap in the bustling swarm. 'Are you all right in there?'

'Of course I'm all right. It's just a bit hard to see.' She stopped nine or ten paces away. 'Eew! What's that all over the ground?'

Joshi related what had happened while she was gone. 'I guess I owe Vindon my life,' he finished.

'That you do, cousin!' Vindon agreed. 'So now I think it's only fair that you and honey bee tell me why you came here.'

Joshi looked at the bee girl — at her eyes, actually, since there wasn't much more of her that he could see. 'What do you think, Abelha? Should we tell him?'

'Why not?' she said. 'If Vindon's coming with us, he's going to find out sooner or later.'

Joshi would have preferred it to be later. Despite his cousin having saved him from the giant hectapus creature, Joshi still didn't trust him. But Abelha was right; Vindon was going to find out anyway. Reluctantly, Joshi told him why they were here.

His cousin doubled over laughing. 'Flowers! We're risking our lives for *flowers!*'

'Not just any flowers,' Joshi said. 'Green flowers. Our family colour.'

Vindon wiped his eyes. 'Here I was thinking you and honey bee must have found a secret treasure map or something,' he said, sounding disappointed.

'If we find any treasure, you'll get a share,' Joshi reminded him.

'There isn't likely to be any treasure, though,' Vindon said sourly. 'Look around you. Do you see any sign of people? I think this place is uninhabited.'

'That depends what you mean by uninhabited,' Abelha countered, her voice muffled by humming bees. 'Look over there.'

The other two turned their heads where she was pointing. Joshi let out a small gasp. 'Is that a … ?' he breathed, wondering if he was dreaming.

Beside him, Abelha whispered, 'Isn't it gorgeous, Joshi!'

The unicorn stood grazing on a ferny knoll about fifty yards away. Not quite horse, not quite antelope, it was as white as the full moon, with a long silver horn sprouting from the centre of its regal forehead. Joshi held his breath. He knew this was a privilege granted to very few people. To see a unicorn was supposed to bring you good luck for the rest of your life. Suddenly the beautiful creature raised its head and looked in their direction. For half a heartbeat it didn't move, then, with a long, graceful bound, it disappeared into the trees.

'I wish I'd brought my crossbow,' Vindon muttered.

'*What?*' said Joshi and Abelha, both at the same time.

'I reckon I could have hit it.'

'You couldn't shoot a unicorn!' Abelha said, shocked.

Vindon picked something out of his teeth. 'It was only fifty yards away,' he said, examining the scrap of food on his fingernail, 'and standing side-on — an easy shot.'

'But *why* would you want to shoot a unicorn?' asked Joshi.

'For the horn,' his cousin said. 'It's supposed to have magical properties. You know what the going price is for a unicorn's horn back at the Fences' Guild? A hundred royals per inch. Per *inch!* That one was easily twenty-four inches long. We could be rich!'

'That's disgusting!' said Abelha.

Vindon looked confused. 'What's disgusting about being rich? It's what everyone wants.'

'Not me, I'm perfectly happy with what I've got,' said the bee girl from within her cloak of bees. She turned and began walking away. 'Come on, you two. Let's find what we came for, then go back to Quentaris.'

As the two cousins followed her into the trees, Vindon paused for a final glance back at the ferny knoll where they'd seen the unicorn. His face flushed with excitement and a scheming grin passed across his lips.

11

The Garden in the Sky

'I don't understand it.' Abelha frowned. 'My bees are going off in all directions, yet we haven't seen any flowers — not even normal-coloured ones.'

It was true. As lush and green as everything was, there didn't seem to be a single flower anywhere in the giant forest. Yet Abelha's worker bees kept buzzing away into the trees and returning with nectar. Several came back with green petals stuck to them.

'It might be because the flowers are green,' suggested Joshi, 'so they're camouflaged among all the other green stuff.'

'You could be right,' the bee girl said thoughtfully.

Her bees no longer covered her. Abelha had placed the honeycomb containing the queen bee and its young in the beaded pouch hanging around her neck; the rest of the swarm dangled from the pouch in a heavy brown and yellow clump, like a papoose. Plucking one out of the air, Abelha tied the insect to another short length of cotton and set it free. They followed it for about forty yards, directly to the base of one of the giant trees. The bee circled once, then flew straight up.

'Know what?' said Vindon, watching the bee twirling at the end of its tether about two feet above Abelha's upturned face. 'I think that's where your green flowers are.'

And he pointed up at the forest canopy, a thousand feet above their heads.

'Who's good at climbing?' Abelha asked.

Joshi felt nauseous and dizzy. *Don't look down!* he kept telling himself, but it was impossible not to. Abelha and Vindon looked like ants. He wished he were waiting down there on the ground with Abelha and Vindon climbing the tree. But, as his cousin had correctly pointed out, Joshi was the one who wanted the green flowers.

Now Joshi was beginning to wonder how much he *really* wanted them. He was about two hundred feet up the tree and he still hadn't seen any flowers. Occasionally a bee would whizz past him, either going straight up, or coming straight down. So the green flowers — if they actually existed — were still above him.

At least the climbing was easier now that Joshi was up among the branches. For the first fifty feet he'd had to scale the huge trunk like a human spider, his body flattened against the bark, his fingertips and bare toes jammed into whatever wrinkles and crannies he could find. He'd had to leave his boots on the ground, and he felt naked without them. A gardener without boots was like a sword-for-hire without a sword. Joshi felt envious of his cousin on the forest floor far below. Vindon not only had his sword (and his boots), he had Abelha for company.

Your girlfriend, Vindon had called her, but Joshi had denied it. They were just friends. In fact, Abelha was Joshi's *only* friend now that he'd finished school and shocked everyone by becoming a gardener. Not that he needed lots of friends, Joshi told himself, when he had the company of all his plants and flowers. He wondered if it was the same for Abelha. Did she have any friends other than him? Or were her bees all the company she needed?

A lone bee circled him on its journey up the tree and Joshi smiled at it. 'Lead the way,' he said, reaching up for the next branch.

The sun had moved halfway down the sky by the time Joshi pulled himself clear of the thin layer of clouds that gathered in the forest canopy. He drew in his breath at what he saw. It felt like being in a fairytale his mother used to read to him as a child. *Jack and the Giant Sweet Pea*, it was called. In the fairytale, Jack climbs above the clouds and finds a giant's castle with treasure inside. There was no castle here, but there *was* treasure. It wasn't conventional treasure, though — not the type that would make Vindon's eyes light up — but to Joshi the sight that greeted him was worth more than all the gold royals in the Archon's vaults.

He was in a garden in the sky!

Rising out of the clouds like waterlilies was a

floating carpet of flowers. They stretched away in all directions, for as far as the eye could see. The air was heavy with their sweet scent. Bees, butterflies and tiny jewel-like hummingbirds darted from one blossom to the next.

Now Joshi understood why they hadn't seen any flowers earlier. They all grew up here — at the very tops of the giant trees. They were skyflowers!

With a trembling hand, he reached for the nearest flower and carefully snapped its thin stem. Tiny dewdrops of mist sparkled on its petals as he lifted it up into the sunshine and for a moment Joshi forgot to breathe.

The flower was bright green.

12

Too Close for Comfort

JOSHI PICKED AS MANY of the green flowers as he
could safely carry in one hand, then he took
one last look around. He could quite happily
have remained in the magical sky garden for the rest
of the day, but to do so would have been foolish.
Already half the afternoon was gone. He had to get
down well before nightfall, so that he and his two
companions could find their way back to the rift
before dark.

Climbing down the giant tree proved to be much
more difficult than climbing up. Joshi could only
use one hand, because he held the precious
skyflowers in the other; and he had to go down
backwards, which meant looking down a lot and

that made him dizzy. It was a long, long, *long* way down.

As the afternoon wore on, the branches became slippery with moisture. The clouds had closed in, wrapping the forest in a dense, grey fog. It was difficult to see more than a few yards in any direction. At least when he looked down, he could no longer see how far it was to fall.

He had to test each branch first. Often they were slippery, or too skinny to take his weight. So when one skidded sideways beneath his heel and slid up over his ankle, Joshi thought nothing of it. He simply moved his foot sideways, searching for another, more stable foothold. But the slippery branch moved sideways, too; almost as if it were following him.

Then it coiled sinuously around his calf.

Joshi gasped and looked down. It wasn't a branch — it was the bronze scaly arm of a hectapus!

For a moment time seemed to stand still. Joshi was frozen in fear. Just his eyes moved and what they observed only compounded his sense of doom. The creature seemed to be everywhere. Its slimy orange body hung six feet below him like some vile, overripe fruit, while the rest of it — a vast tangle of impossibly long, boneless tentacles — was knotted around almost every branch in sight; some even disappeared all the way around the massive tree trunk. But its body was the worst part. The small fish-like eyes were fixed hungrily on Joshi, and its toothy mouth opened and closed with a wet hissing and clicking sound.

Finally Joshi recovered enough of his senses to move. At least, he *tried* to move. Dragging upwards against the grip of the hectapus, he twirled his leg in a desperate attempt to unwind the horrid thing wrapped around it. But the hectapus held on. The grotesque mouth-like orifices along the underside of its tentacle seemed to suck at his skin, even through the coarse fabric of his trousers, making it impossible to shake off. And Joshi was unable to kick it with his other foot, for fear of falling. He had only one hand and one leg to hang on with, and the ground was still a long, long way down. Three more of the creature's scaly tentacles came slithering up through the branches and leaves towards him, like blind, questing snakes. He had to do something. Fast.

Almost too late, Joshi remembered his pruning knife. He carried it in a small leather sheath permanently attached to his belt. But how could he get it out? His right hand gripped the stout branch above his head, his left hand held the skyflowers. To let go with one meant certain death, to let go with the other meant losing the skyflowers. For a second, Joshi considered the second option. The flowers would fall *down*, after all, and that's the direction he was going. But what if they became caught in some branches lower down and he couldn't find them?

They were skyflowers, *green* flowers — he'd risked too much to lose them now.

But was he prepared to lose his life for them?

Another of the hectapus's tentacles snaked up towards him. Joshi took all his weight with his right arm and kicked wildly at the quivering bronze limb with his free leg. Missed! The tentacle whipped out of the way; then, quick as lightning, it flicked around his ankle. Now the creature had him by both legs. Joshi's full weight, as well as the heavy pull of the hectapus, dragged against his straining right arm. His muscles quivered and ached, but to let go would be suicidal. The hectapus was just below him. He could hear its deadly teeth clattering like knife blades; he could feel its warm, fetid breath on the bare soles of his feet. Joshi was too scared to look down and meet the creature's merciless silver eyes, or to face its snapping, slavering jaws, but wherever he looked he saw its long, scaly tentacles revolving slowly around branches like ropes sliding through pulleys, as the vile creature inched closer and closer. The hectapus was dragging itself upwards and dragging Joshi down. He felt his right hand starting to slip.

He had no choice.

But he couldn't drop the skyflowers!

Instead, Joshi clamped their stems between his teeth and reached for his pruning knife. *Slash! Slash!* With two swipes of its razor-sharp blade, Joshi severed the tentacles that held his legs. Purple liquid sprayed everywhere. But immediately after the damaged tentacles fell away, three more took their place. Then a fourth flashed up, coming straight at his face. Joshi jerked his head sideways. Narrowly missing its target, the long sinuous tentacle wrapped itself around the skyflowers.

Joshi was not conscious of dropping his pruning knife, but suddenly it was no longer in his hand. In its place, Joshi was holding the stems of the skyflowers, having a tug-of-war with the hectapus. The creature was strong, but Joshi was determined. He gritted his teeth, his whole body quivered with the strain. Slowly, the tentacle lost its grip on the green stems, then there was a loud hiss from somewhere below him and the tentacle unwound and fell away altogether.

The tentacles around his legs also let go.

Joshi blinked the sweat out of his eyes. He was hanging one-handed from the branch. Below him, for just a second, he saw the hectapus. It was curled up in a huge knot like a hundred tangled snakes. Through a gap in the twisted tentacles, Joshi had a last glimpse of its hateful silver eyes. Directly below one of them, buried up to its worn wooden handle, was Joshi's pruning knife.

Then, with a last hissing gasp, the creature let go altogether and tumbled down into the mist, bouncing from branch to branch, trailing its tentacles like long wet ropes until it disappeared from sight.

Joshi lowered himself to the branch below him and sat there for several minutes, regaining his breath and trying to stop himself from shaking. *That was much too close for comfort*, he thought.

But he'd won. He'd beaten the hectapus fair and square, as well as saving the skyflowers.

Then he looked at the flowers and his elation left him like an escaped breath.

He was holding a bunch of long green stems. All
the leaves — and all but one of the skyflowers —
had been stripped off them. And the flower that
remained had lost more than half of its green petals.

Joshi sat on the branch, sadly studying the
single, bedraggled green flower, and considered
whether or not he had time to climb all the way
back up to the top of the giant tree for more.

That was when he heard a distant, piercing
scream.

13

Blood!

THE CRY CAME FROM below him. It was a whole octave higher than Vindon's scream earlier in the day, when he'd come face to face with the bear. It could only be one person: Abelha.

Then Joshi had a horrifying thought. The hectapus had fallen on her!

Stuffing the skyflower roughly inside his tunic — and ignoring the possibility that the hectapus might not have been alone — Joshi began swinging down through the damp, slippery branches like a circus orang-u-man.

He'd been higher up than he thought, still four or five hundred feet from the ground. Even so, Joshi made the descent in only a few minutes.

Leaving the last of the branches, he slithered down the final fifty feet of bare bark in a terrifying, nail-tearing slide. He hit the ground hard, with a jarring thump that clunked his teeth together and buckled his knees. Joshi collapsed in a heap, all the wind knocked out of him. But he was back on his feet in a matter of moments, gasping for breath and casting around for Abelha and Vindon.

The hectapus lay in a tangled heap about ten feet out from the tree trunk, but there was no sign of Joshi's two companions.

'Abelha?' he said tentatively. Then he raised his voice. '*Abelha! Vindon! Where are you?*'

There was no answer. Where could they be? Joshi turned in a circle, then he limped right around the tree, in the forlorn hope that they might be around the other side. Hiding from him, perhaps. Playing a game. But Vindon wasn't the type to play games. And Abelha wouldn't remain hidden when she heard the fear and concern in Joshi's voice.

They aren't answering, he told himself, *because they aren't here!*

Remembering Abelha's terrified scream, Joshi wondered if something had chased them away. Or

— worse — if something had *taken* them away. His skin prickled.

Joshi's boots and socks sat side by side next to the tree trunk, exactly where he'd left them. Quickly he pulled them on. Then he limped over to the hectapus and retrieved his knife, wiping its blade clean on a tuft of grass.

That was when he noticed the bees. The ground was littered with them. Most were dead, but a few still fluttered their wings weakly, or scurried in slow, aimless circles through the trampled grass. All had their stingers ripped out. Joshi felt sick. Something bad had happened here.

'Abelha! Vindon!' he called again. But not so loud this time; he was afraid of what else might be out in the forest, listening to him. Perhaps even watching him. He shivered nervously.

A bee buzzed past Joshi's ear. He spun around and followed it with his eyes. The insect circled the ground where most of the dead and dying bees lay, then flew away through the trees. Another bee came flying down out of the trees overhead. After circling its fallen sisters five or six times, it too flew off into the forest. Both bees had gone in the same direction. Holding his pruning knife in a white-knuckled grip, Joshi set out after them.

He had only gone a few paces when a flash of colour caught his eye. He bent down for a closer look. A tiny jewel of red liquid clung to a grass stem. Blood!

A few yards further on, Joshi found another red droplet lying on a fallen leaf. Then a bright smear across the stem of a vine. The blood trail led him in the same direction as the bees.

Joshi started running.

14

Chasing *it*

THE TRAIL LED HIM deep into the forest. It was easy to follow. Whoever was bleeding (Joshi hoped with all his heart that it wasn't Abelha) was dripping blood at regular intervals. Every five or six yards, he came across another drop on a leaf, on a tree root, or smeared across a fern. They were only small drops, but Joshi wondered how far you could go if you were losing blood like that.

And he wondered *where* they were going. Was something chasing them? That seemed the most logical explanation. Whatever had made Abelha scream, was now chasing her and Vindon through the forest. And Joshi was chasing *it!*

He wondered what *it* was. Another hectapus, perhaps. Or even the giant bear. He didn't care, so long as he caught up with it before it caught up with Abelha. Pruning knife clutched firmly in his fist, Joshi felt ready to take on anything if it meant saving the bee girl.

But he wasn't ready for what confronted him when finally he caught up with his quarry. Crashing out of the undergrowth like a wild boar pursued by a pack of hounds, Joshi skidded to a halt. He was standing at the edge of a clearing. Fifteen yards away, with his back to Joshi, stood Vindon. Sword in hand, he seemed to be threatening Abelha, who was crouched in some ferns. A swarm of bees formed a buzzing wall between them, partially obscuring the girl from Joshi's view and preventing Vindon from moving forward.

'Wh-what's happening?' stammered Joshi, lowering his knife.

When Vindon turned his head, Joshi scarcely recognised him. One eye was swollen completely shut and the rest of his face was a palette of livid red blotches and ugly purple weals. 'Gonna kill 'er,' he slurred through thick, puffy lips.

Joshi raised his knife again. 'You'll have to kill me first!'

His cousin laughed, or tried to — it sounded more like a wheeze. Then he shrugged. 'I thould kill 'er,' he lisped, 'after what th-ee done to me. But tell yer what, garden boy. You talk some thense into yer girlfriend — make 'er give me what'th mine — an' I'll let bygone-th be bygone-th.'

Abelha spoke for the first time. 'It isn't yours, Vindon.'

'Ith tho! I thaw it first. Would have got it, too, if you hadn't thcreamed an thcared it off.'

Joshi tried to see through the mist of bees. The bee girl was crouched over a yellowish shape half hidden among the ferns. 'What have you got there, Abelha?'

'I don't know. It's an animal of some kind. Vindon tried to kill it.'

'It'th a golden mink,' said Vindon. 'Worth ten royal-th back at the fur market.'

Finally Joshi was beginning to understand what had happened. 'Did you injure it?' he asked. 'Is that what made the blood trail?'

'Came walking right up to uth, bold ath brath,' said Vindon. 'I had it cold, but yer utheleth girl-friend thcreamed an' it jumped outta the way of my thord. Tho I only winged it. Then the utheleth wench thet her bee-th on me.'

'You would have killed it otherwise,' Abelha said.

He nodded. 'I *am* gunna kill it! I thaw it first — that make-th it mine.'

'It isn't anyone's,' Joshi said, surprising himself. 'It's a wild animal. Let me have a look at it, Abelha.'

She murmured something to her bees and they allowed him through. Abelha no longer wore her papoose of bees; those that weren't involved in keeping Vindon away clustered in a heavy clump to her hessian pouch, hanging from the small bush beside her. Joshi approached warily and crouched on her other side. The wounded animal lay in a bed of ferns, its sides heaving, its sapphire blue eyes staring up at them in mute terror as Abelha held a bloodied handkerchief to its quivering flank. Joshi had never seen a golden mink before. It looked a bit like a marten, only larger — it was the size of a dog fox — and its fur was thicker, glossier and golden in colour; it almost matched Abelha's hair. Joshi could see why these creatures were so prized by fur traders. But this one, he vowed, would never be turned into a fur coat.

'Let's see what he's done to you,' Joshi said softly, lifting Abelha's handkerchief from the wound.

It wasn't as bad as he'd feared. Vindon's sword had struck the mink a glancing blow just behind the ribcage, inflicting a long jagged gash in the creature's velvet skin, but barely penetrating the muscle beneath. There was a lot of blood though, and the animal seemed to be in shock. Joshi replaced the balled-up handkerchief on the wound and instructed Abelha to hold it firmly in place, then he crossed to the edge of the clearing and entered the forest.

It didn't take him long to find what he was looking for. Trailing across the exposed roots of one of the giant trees was a thin, spidery vine with leaves shaped like spears. Dragonwort. The same plant grew in Quentaris; any gardener would know it. But few knew the medicinal properties of the dragonwort's knobbly, yam-like roots. A healer had told Joshi about it, in exchange for some advice on growing everlasting-life daisies. Joshi traced the meandering vine to its source and dug down with his pruning knife. Unearthing a fat tuber, he wet his finger with spittle and wiped most of the dirt off it. Then he popped the root into his mouth.

'Are you *eating* something?' Abelha asked when Joshi returned from the forest.

He crouched next to her and spat a wad of

chewed, green pulp into his palm. 'Dragonwort,' he explained as he spread the healing salve over the wound. 'It'll stop the bleeding and take the pain away.'

Almost immediately, the mink stopped trembling. It lifted its head and licked Joshi's wrist. He gently stroked its feather-soft fur.

'Joshi, you're amazing,' whispered Abelha.

He shrugged modestly. 'No I'm not. I'm just a gardener.'

Vindon had been sitting watching them from the other side of the screen of bees. Now he rose to his feet, unsheathing his sword as he did so.

'Doan like to interrupt you two lovebird-th,' he slurred. 'But we got company.'

Joshi and Abelha turned in the direction he was looking. And, like Vindon, they too rose slowly to their feet.

'Holy Mushin!' breathed Joshi.

Stalking towards them was another golden mink. But while this one was roughly the same colour and shape as the one lying in the ferns at their feet, in certain other respects — notably size and ferocity — it bore a frightening resemblance to a timber wolf. Or a lion.

'I thought *this* was how big they got,' whispered

Abelha, referring to the injured one.

'So did I,' admitted Joshi. 'But I guess it's just a baby. This must be its mother.'

'She doesn't look happy.'

'She thinks we've hurt her baby.'

The adult golden mink was twenty feet away, slinking towards them with its teeth bared and making a low growling sound in its throat.

'Back away from her,' Joshi whispered. 'Really slowly.'

They started backing away. Abelha scooped the clump of bees out of the bush as they went past. Sensing a new and greater threat to the bee girl, the other bees abandoned their guard on Vindon and buzzed angrily around the giant mink's head. The animal snarled in annoyance and batted at the swarming insects with its front paws. None of them stung it — they were awaiting Abelha's command. Instead, the bee girl hummed to them, calling them back, and allowed the mother mink to reach her kitten.

Watching the humans warily with her sapphire blue eyes, the giant mink lifted her young one by the nape of its neck, turned and went trotting off into the forest.

'Did yer ever thee anything tho beautiful?'

gasped Vindon. He stood at Joshi's elbow, sword in hand, and stared with his one good eye at the spot where the two golden animals had disappeared.

Joshi turned to him in surprise. 'They were pretty magnificent, weren't they?'

An expression close to rapture lit up his cousin's horribly disfigured face. 'Back in other land-th,' he lisped through swollen lips, 'them minkth only grow big ath cat-th. But you could make a whole fur coat from jutht that thingle mother one.'

'Vindon Nibhelline, you make me sick,' said Abelha.

He narrowed his single eye at her. 'You better watch yer back, honey bee. Or thomething bad might happen ...'

His timing was perfect. Almost as if it had been awaiting this cue, a mighty roar shook the air and a great, shaggy animal the size of a house came thundering out of the forest.

15

Not Th-o Tough

ABELHA'S BEES DIDN'T WAIT for her command; they swarmed to her defence like an army protecting its citadel. But they were only bees — it would have taken a real army to stop the giant bear. Rising up on its hind legs, it advanced across the clearing like something out of Joshi's worst nightmare.

But this wasn't a nightmare, it was real.

The bear was almost on them; it seemed to fill half the sky. At the first sight of it, Vindon had turned tail and fled. Joshi grabbed Abelha's hand and tried to follow him, but the bee girl twisted free of his grip and turned to face the monster. She began humming to her bees, ordering them to flee, but they couldn't hear her above the roaring of the bear; and anyway Abelha's safety was more important to them than their lives. They concentrated their attack on the massive creature's head, gathering in two boiling clusters around its eyes, preventing it from seeing. Clawing at its face, the giant bear bellowed in rage. It lumbered in a blind half-circle, then sat down.

'Abelha, come *on!*' screamed Joshi, catching hold of her wrist. 'We've got to get to the trees. It's our only hope.'

Once again she tried to pull away from him, but this time Joshi held on. He couldn't allow her to remain there and die with her bees. 'I'm sorry about this,' he muttered and lifted the bee girl, kicking and protesting, off the ground, and slung her over his shoulder. Abelha cursed and fought and kicked her legs wildly, but Joshi just held her all the harder. He was much stronger than her and both their lives were at stake. The bees could only delay the giant bear for a few more moments, then it would come after them. Ignoring Abelha's struggles and indignant cries of protest, Joshi staggered across the clearing and into the trees.

After a few hundred yards, Abelha went limp on his shoulder. 'You can put me down now,' she said dully.

Joshi set the bee girl on the ground, but he kept hold of one hand. He tried leading her deeper into the forest. 'Come on, Abelha. We've got to keep going,' he urged.

She pulled the other way. 'It won't come after us. It only wanted the honey.'

'What honey?'

Abelha sniffed. Her face was streaked with lines of damp pollen and tears. 'Every time I take the bees from one of my hives, I bring a bit of honeycomb with me — for the queen bee and her babies to live in. It was in my carry-pouch, but the strap broke when you lifted me.'

Joshi felt awful. 'I'm really sorry, Abelha. But I couldn't leave you there — the bear would have killed you.'

'Probably.' Her eyes welled up, her lower lip started to tremble. 'But my poor bees!'

She put her head against his chest and began weeping. Joshi wasn't sure what to do. Tentatively, he slid his arms around her, and Abelha pressed against the front of his tunic.

'Well, well, well!' said a familiar, slurring voice, and Vindon stepped out from behind a tree. 'Isn' thith a very touching little thene!'

Joshi scowled at him over the top of Abelha's

bent head. 'Shut your mouth, you useless coward!'

Vindon's bloated, discoloured face turned an even deeper shade of purple and one hand dropped to the hilt of his sword. 'Better wat-th who you call a coward, garden boy. I might have to teath you a bit of rethpect.'

'Like you taught that bear a bit of respect, I suppose?' Joshi sneered. 'One look at it and you ran away like a frightened rabbit!'

Vindon dropped his one-eyed gaze to the ground just in front of him. 'A thord's no good against thomething that thize,' he murmured. 'Anyway, I thaved you from that hectaputh, remember?'

Joshi did remember. 'Sorry, Vindon. I guess we shouldn't be mouthing off at each other. Like Abelha said, this is a pretty dangerous place and we ought to stick together if we want to get back to Quentaris in one piece.'

'Yeah, well,' Vindon said. 'Tell your girlfriend that if you two want the protection of me an' my thord, th-ee can't pull any more thtunt-th like th-ee did before with her bee-th.'

At this, Abelha extricated herself from Joshi's arms. 'You don't have to worry about that, Vindon — I no longer have any bees.'

He looked surprised. 'Why not? Whath happened to them?'

The bee girl wiped her eyes and took a deep, shuddering breath. 'The bear killed them,' she whispered.

'Commitheration-th,' said Vindon, but he didn't look or sound sorry at all. In fact, he seemed pleased. He thrust his chest out and narrowed his one good eye to an inscrutable squint. 'When you two athked me along on thith little adventure,' he said thoughtfully, 'you thaid I'd get a thare in anything we find, didn't you?'

'Only if it was gold or treasure,' Joshi corrected him.

Vindon tapped his fingers on his sword handle. 'You tricked me. You knew all along there *wathn't* gold or treathure here. What you came looking for wath your prethith green flower-th, wathn't it?'

'That's ... true,' admitted Joshi.

'Did you find any?'

For the first time since he'd climbed down the giant tree, Joshi remembered the flower he'd saved from the hectapus. He undid his top button and carefully pulled out the long bent stem with its single, battered green flower.

Vindon raised his swollen eyebrows. 'Ith *that* what we rithked our live-th for?'

'It's *green!*' Joshi said. 'The Nibhelline family colour. I'll be famous.'

Too late, he realised what he had just said.

'*Who'll* be famous, couthin?' Vindon asked dangerously. In one smooth movement, he slid his sword from its scabbard and pressed it against Joshi's chest. Taken by surprise, Joshi stepped backwards and bumped into the wall-like trunk of a giant tree.

'Leave him alone!' Abelha cried. She flew at Vindon, but he lashed out with his elbow, knocking her to the ground.

'Not th-o tough without your little inthect friend-th to help you, are you honey bee?' he sneered.

Joshi trembled with barely suppressed rage, but there was nothing he could do. 'You're a spineless coward, Vindon, for hitting an unarmed girl.'

Vindon pressed a little harder with his sword. '*Who'th* a thpineleth coward, garden boy?'

'You are. I'll bet you haven't even got the guts to kill me.'

'Joshi! Just give him the flower!' Abelha appealed to him from the ground.

'No.' He firmed his jaw and looked Vindon squarely in his one good eye. 'If you want the flower, cousin, you'll have to kill me first.'

Vindon let out a loud guffaw. That was a mistake. Because his left eye was swollen completely closed, his nose (also badly swollen) obstructed his view of Joshi's right side from the waist down. And when he laughed, Vindon's head rocked back several degrees, obstructing his view even more. He didn't see Joshi's hand snatch the pruning knife out of its leather sheath. Nor did he see its short steel blade flash up and knock his sword out of the way of Joshi's right leg, which was swinging up towards his now unguarded lower body with the force of a battering ram.

When Vindon came to, he lay doubled up on the ground in considerable pain, looking up at the wrong end of his own sword.

'Consider yourself released of your duties, cousin,' Joshi said. 'Abelha and I no longer require a sword-for-hire.'

16

A Good Fairytale

'YOU CAN'T JUTHT LEAVE me!' Vindon protested, limping through the forest behind them. 'Thith plathe is teeming with all thort-th of wild animal-th. I could get killed!'

'That'd be a shame,' Joshi said dispassionately.

Vindon's hideously swollen face trembled with emotion. 'I'm your couthin! How can you be th-o heartleth?'

'Heartless, am I?' asked Joshi. 'Who was the one who maimed a defenceless baby mink? Who wants to sell these lovely old trees for firewood? Who's prepared to kill *unicorns*?'

'I didn' mean it. I wath jutht joking.'

'Tell the baby mink that,' Abelha snorted.

'Very well, I admit it,' wailed Vindon. 'I did hurt that on purpoth. It wath cruel an' mean an' heartleth, and I'm very, very thorry. I won't do it again.'

Joshi glanced over his shoulder. 'Do you promise?'

'Yeth. I promith.'

'And if we let you come with us, do you promise not to make any more trouble?'

'I promith.'

'Okay, you can come,' said Joshi. He held out his hand. 'Give me your belt.'

'My belt?' Vindon's good eye nearly popped out of his head. 'Why do you want my belt?'

'Because I need the scabbard to put this sword in. It's getting heavy.'

'Give it back then.'

'I'm not that stupid,' Joshi laughed. 'Come on, get your belt off.'

'But my breech-th will fall down!' Vindon protested.

Abelha giggled, but Joshi was careful to keep his own voice serious. 'Just give me the scabbard then. I don't think Abelha and I are quite ready for the sight of your undergarments.'

A moment ago, Joshi had said he wasn't stupid. But he couldn't help thinking, as Vindon grudgingly removed his scabbard and tossed it to him, that allowing his cousin to come with them was probably a decision he was going to regret.

Joshi and Vindon crouched among the ferns at the edge of the forest, watching Abelha creep slowly out into the clearing.

'The bear'th probably lying in wait for her,' whispered Vindon.

'It's gone,' Joshi said softly, sounding much more confident than he felt. What if his cousin was right? Abelha's bees were all dead — it would be up to Joshi to protect her. He had the sword. But what good was a sword, he asked himself, against a creature as large and ferocious as the giant bear?

Vindon must have guessed the direction of his thoughts. 'A croth-bow would do the job,' he whispered. 'One thot between the eyeth, an' you'd have a bearthkin rug worth a fortune.'

'Vindon, you promised to stop all this talk about killing things.'

'You can th-top me from talking, but you can't th-top me from thinking.'

Joshi knew it was pointless trying to reason with him. His cousin was right; you couldn't control someone's thoughts. Just as you couldn't control the type of person they were. Vindon was untrustworthy to the core. He had no intention of keeping his promise. It was a mistake to have led him to this beautiful, yet dangerous world. Joshi and Abelha should have made sure they weren't being followed when they first ventured into Deadly Cave. Because of their carelessness, Vindon had found the rift. And now that he knew where it was — and what lay beyond it — he would come back, bringing others like him: hunters, trappers and tree-fellers, who would plunder the aeons-old forest, killing and destroying everything that could be taken away and sold. Vindon was going to become a very, very rich man and there was nothing Joshi could do to stop him.

Out in the clearing, Abelha had begun gathering dead bees.

'What'th th-ee doing?' asked Vindon.

'You'll see,' Joshi said, unable to shake off the deep sense of dread that had fallen over him. He had tried to talk her out of it, but Abelha had insisted. She *had* to come back to the clearing, she'd told him. She had to send her bees to their final resting place.

'But will they hear you?' Joshi had asked. 'This isn't Quentaris.'

The bee girl had pointed up at the forest canopy high above them, where the late afternoon sun poked a single weak strand of golden light through the leaves and the clouds. 'It's the same sky,' she'd said.

Now she knelt in the centre of the clearing, with a thousand dead bees in the scoop of her dress, and another four or five thousand scattered around her, and from deep within her lungs came the same slow, lilting hum Joshi had first heard three days ago in the abandoned marketplace.

'What'th th-ee ... ?' Vindon whispered, but Joshi shushed him.

'Listen,' he said quietly.

Now there was a sound like distant hoofbeats. Slowly it grew louder and became a dull roar that made the very air pulsate. An eerie yellow twilight fell over the clearing. Vindon glanced at Joshi, a fearful look in his one good eye, then he followed his cousin's upturned gaze. An eerie orange glow, like an early sunset, had moved across the sky. Slowly it settled among the cloudy treetops, then it came through them, turning the clouds orange and spinning them around in a churning whirlwind that stripped a million leaves from the branches and created such a roar that Joshi and Vindon covered their ears. Moments later, the belly of the storm wound itself into a long yellow tornado that came spiralling slowly down towards the forest floor, where the small, lone figure of Abelha waited.

'Ghoth-t bees!' cried Vindon, involuntarily gripping his cousin's arm. 'Yer girlfriend better run. Th-ee'll be killed!'

'She knows what she's doing,' Joshi shouted back. 'They only want their dead.'

As the huge howling swarm descended, one of the ghost bees separated from the spinning throng. It flew directly to the thicket where the cousins lay in hiding. Joshi held his breath. He could feel Vindon trembling beside him. The small yet terrifying apparition hovered just above them, no more than a foot away. It was the size of a normal bee, but it glowed like molten bronze. Where its eyes should have been, there were just two black holes. Yet it was watching them, Joshi could tell. Sizing them up. He didn't dare move. From the corner of his eye, he saw Abelha turn her head in their direction. The bee girl was kneeling directly below the spinning funnel of the whirlwind; her long hair danced around her in a wild golden tangle, her clothing whipped and flayed. She crooked a finger at the ghost bee above Joshi's head. It hesitated a moment, then turned and zipped back into the howling storm that finally hid Abelha completely from Joshi's view.

It was impossible to see what happened next. The wind was too strong and there was too much flying debris. Joshi had to close his eyes and cover his head with his arms. His world was reduced to a deafening, buzzing roar. It became difficult to breathe. All he could do was flatten himself to the ground and try not to be blown away.

It ended with surprising suddenness. Joshi hadn't been aware of a lessening in the din, or an abating of the wind, until the whirlwind was gone altogether. There was silence. Cautiously, he raised his head. The ghost bees were gone. Everything was perfectly still. Peaceful, almost. At the centre of the clearing, Abelha climbed slowly to her feet. Her face was deathly pale and streaked with fresh tears. She straightened her clothing and brushed the hair out of her eyes.

'Are you all right?' Joshi asked, hurrying towards her.

She quickly wiped her eyes. 'I'm fine. What about you? I should have told you to wait farther back in the trees.'

'I'm all right,' Joshi said, picking a leaf out of her tangled hair. He wanted to hug her, but knew Vindon was watching. 'Weren't you scared?' he whispered.

'Of the ghost bees?' She shook her head. 'All they wanted were their dead sisters.'

Joshi looked around him. Not a single dead bee remained. 'Where did they take them?'

'I don't know. Up into the sky. My grandmother — she was a beekeeper, too — she says they turn into flowers, but that sounds like a fairytale to me.'

Joshi smiled. It reminded him of the skyflower tucked inside his vest. 'It sounds like a good fairy-tale,' he said.

There was a rustling from the ferns behind him and Vindon came limping out. 'I'll tell you a *bad* fairytale,' he growled. 'Three Quentaran-th in a

122

foretht filled with all kind-th of nath-ty, danger-outh animal-th, an' it get-th dark before they find their way back to the rift.'

Joshi surveyed the treetops high above them. Vindon was right — it was almost dusk. If they didn't get back to the hollow tree before it grew dark, they would have to spend the night here. At the mercy of the hectapuses, the giant bears, the giant minks and who knew what other strange and terrifying creatures that roamed this unexplored world.

'Does anyone *know* the way back?' he asked nervously.

17

So Brave!

THEY FOLLOWED ABELHA. SHE claimed to know
the way.

'Bees never get lost,' she explained. 'And
I've watched how they do it.'

Joshi hoped she was right. Night was falling fast,
and the trees and bushes around them seemed to be
closing in with the descending shadows. Nothing
looked familiar. Yet Abelha walked confidently
ahead, as if she was taking a Highday afternoon
stroll. Joshi had to trust that they were going in the
right direction. He followed close behind her, his
eyes darting to and fro, his hand on his sword
pommel. He considered it his sword now, not
Vindon's, and the weight of it, swinging from his
hip, was reassuring. Even so, it didn't feel quite

right to be wearing a sword. He was a gardener, not a swordsman, and he wasn't sure how effective he would be if he had to use it. The spectre of Taschia Duelph still haunted him. *Beaten by a thirteen-year-old girl!* He would have been more comfortable had Vindon been in charge of the sword. But his cousin couldn't be trusted.

'Th-ee'th leading uth in thircle-th!' Vindon grumbled behind him.

Joshi didn't bother turning around. 'Stop complaining, Vindon. She knows where she's going.'

But did she? Joshi was beginning to have doubts himself. 'Abelha?' he whispered. 'Is it much farther?'

She stopped and turned to answer him.

And that's when the hectapus struck.

What had looked like a shadowy vine trailing from an overhanging branch of a small tree, suddenly sprang into life and wrapped itself three times around Abelha's waist. It lifted her off her feet even before she had time to scream. Another tentacle flashed down and caught her by the arm. Dangling like a rag doll, Abelha kicked a third tentacle away. Another came twisting down one of its fellow tentacles and slithered, snake-like, around her neck. Abelha clawed at it with her free hand, tearing the ghastly thing off. One came too close to her face; she arched her neck and bit it. But there were too many of them. Despite her valiant struggles, Abelha was being drawn steadily up into the tree. Already she was four feet off the ground.

All this had happened in the space of a few heartbeats. Joshi stood rooted to the spot, too shocked and surprised to move.

'Joshi, help!' cried the terrified girl.

It was all the prompting he needed. Rushing foward, he dragged the sword from its scabbard and aimed a mighty blow at the writhing limbs of the hectapus. But he had to check his swing at the last moment for fear of hitting Abelha. The sword flashed harmlessly below her and buried itself in a tree trunk. Joshi wrenched it free and spun around. Abelha was above his head now, entangled in a dark knot of twisting tentacles. She wasn't screaming, but he could hear her desperate, sobbing breath as she struggled to free herself from the hideous creature. Joshi cocked his right arm, raising the sword high behind his head. But in the failing light, it was difficult to see which limbs belonged to the girl and which belonged to the hectapus.

'Go on, kill the thing!' urged Vindon, hiding behind a thicket.

It was useless advice. How could Joshi kill the hectapus without harming Abelha? She and it were braided together like a single, squirming creature.

'Joshi!' she gasped through a gap in its tentacles.

There was only one thing to do. Joshi opened his arms wide and presented himself to the hectapus tangled all through the branches above him.

'Come on, you cowardly piece of pig's intestine!' he challenged it. 'Take me, too!'

Almost as if it could understand him, the creature sent two long scaly tentacles snaking down. One coiled around Joshi's sword arm, the other looped around his chest. Joshi didn't struggle. *Not yet!* he cautioned himself. With the sword dangling uselessly from his right hand, he forced himself to remain limp as the creature lifted him up. More tentacles wrapped themselves around him: two more around his body, another one around his right arm. He gripped the sword tighter. Joshi was several feet above the ground now, being pulled slowly upwards. *Don't resist!* he reminded himself. *Not yet!* His right hand was growing numb; there was a tingling sensation all the way up to his shoulder.

Too late, Joshi realised what was happening. The hectapus was squeezing his sword arm, trying to make him drop the weapon.

'Oh, you clever thing!' he muttered, as he lost all feeling in his hand and heard the sword hit the ground eight or ten feet below him.

He was right up next to Abelha now. She was still kicking and struggling somewhere inside a great spaghetti of writhing tentacles. Joshi remained limp. It required all his will power. He was damp with sweat and quaking in fear, but he refused to panic. His left arm was still free. He let himself be lifted up past Abelha, right up into the shadowy foliage of the tree.

Joshi heard it before he saw it. From just above him came the clicking rattle of teeth and the slow hiss of expelled breath. It was very dark in the tree; all he could see was a large, pear-shaped silhouette and the greedy silver glint of the hectapus's eyes as it pulled him inexorably towards its mouth.

Still Joshi didn't struggle. He waited until he was less than two feet from the creature's slavering jaws, then he reached across with his left hand, pulled his pruning knife from its sheath and plunged it, with all his strength, dead centre between the glinting eyes.

The hectapus didn't drop them. Rather, it slowly uncoiled its tentacles, lowering Joshi and Abelha almost gently to the ground. Joshi was on his feet in a moment. He helped Abelha up and led her quickly away from the tree. And not a moment too soon. The hectapus landed in a large black heap exactly where they'd been standing, its lifeless tentacles spilling away from it like a giant ball of wool unravelling.

'Thank you, Joshi,' Abelha whispered, hugging him. 'That was *so* brave!'

He tried to stop himself from trembling. 'I had to save you, otherwise who would have led us back to the rift?' he joked.

She turned her face up to his. 'Well! And I thought it was because you liked me.'

'Actually, I d …' Joshi began, but he was interrupted by a slurring voice behind him.

'Th-top playing the big hero, Jothephine! Why don't you tell honey bee how you got whipped by a thirteen-year-old girl?'

Joshi let go of Abelha and spun around. 'I warned you not to call me that!' he growled, raising his fists.

'Th-o you did, Jothephine,' Vindon mocked him. 'But I wouldn't be threatening me if I were you. In fact, I think it'th time thomeone taught you a lethon.'

Gleaming dully in the last pale light of the dying day, the tip of Vindon's sword wavered just a few inches from Joshi's face.

18

Run!

'PUT THAT THING DOWN, Vindon,' Abelha growled. 'We haven't got time for this. If we don't get back through the rift before dark, we'll have to spend the night here.'

Vindon nodded and took a careful step backwards. But he kept the sword raised. 'Very well. But don't think thith ith over, garden boy,' he spat. 'Thoon ath we're back in Quentarith, I'm gonna pay you back for everything you've done to me.'

'I'm looking forward to it,' Joshi said evenly.

His cousin sniggered. He made a threatening gesture with his sword. 'Take yer belt off, Jothephine.'

Wordlessly, Joshi removed the scabbard from his belt and tossed it onto the ground at his cousin's feet.

'Pick it up!' Vindon snarled.

'Pick it up yourself,' said Joshi, turning his back on him. 'Let's go, Abelha. Something around here makes me sick to my stomach — and I'm not talking about the hectapus.'

It was fully dark by the time they reached the hollow log. Joshi located the torch and held it while Vindon used his flint to make a flame. The cousins weren't talking to each other. They communicated through Abelha.

'Tell garden boy to lead the way.'

'Is wet britches scared of the dark?'

'Oh, for goodness sake!' groaned Abelha. She reached for the torch. 'Here, give that to me. *I'll* lead the way.'

But they had only ventured twenty feet into the cavernous hollow log when they heard a noise somewhere in the darkness ahead. It sounded like slow, deep breathing. Wordlessly, they turned round and tiptoed back outside. They took refuge behind some ferns.

'What ith it?' hissed Vindon, straining his eyes into the gaping black maw of the hollow log.

'The bear, I think,' Abelha whispered. 'Sounds like it's asleep.'

'What are we going to do?' asked Joshi.

'I guess we'll have to wait till it comes out.'

Joshi looked behind them. His skin prickled. The forest was pitch black. Anything could be out there in the darkness, watching them. 'But it mightn't come out till daylight,' he whispered.

'We can find somewhere to hide,' said Abelha. 'Maybe we could climb a tree or something.'

'Hectapuses live in trees,' Joshi reminded her.

She raised the guttering torch and all three of them looked nervously up into the maze of shadowy branches above them.

'Well, has anybody got a better suggestion?' Abelha asked after a few moments.

'Let'th thmoke it out,' Vindon lisped.

The girl shook her head. 'I don't think that's a very good idea.'

'Why not?'

'You might make it angry,' she said.

Joshi surprised both of them — and himself — by taking his cousin's side. 'Who cares?' he whispered. 'We can scare it off with fire. It burned its nose last time, so if we all have flaming sticks it won't dare come near us.'

Working quickly and silently, they made a big mound of sticks and dead branches in the mouth of the hollow log. They positioned it to one side of the entrance, so the bear could get past when it came out. When the pile was nearly as tall as them, Abelha set it alight. They waited for the flames to take hold, then Joshi and Vindon piled armfuls of wet leaf-litter and green fern fronds on top, creating a heavy pall of greyish white smoke. But most of the smoke curled up out of the log and drifted off into the night; very little went into the log where it was supposed to.

'I've got an idea,' Vindon said. He ducked outside and returned with two large fern fronds. 'Fan-th,' he explained, handing one to Joshi.

While Abelha stood guard with the flaming torch, the two cousins used the fern fronds to fan the smoke into the depths of the enormous cave-like log.

For a long time nothing happened. A steady stream of smoke disappeared into the hollow, but there was no change in the sound of the bear's deep, slow breathing. The huge creature was still fast asleep. Several times they had to rebuild the fire and place more greenery and leaf-litter on it. They took turns holding the torch, which gave each of them a rest from fanning the smoke. When it was his turn to stand guard, Joshi wasn't sure which direction to face — into the log where the giant bear slept peacefully on, or out of the log's cavernous entrance, where a host of hectapuses might be gathering unseen in the pitch-black night.

A sudden rumble of thunder helped him make up his mind. It came from inside the log, which didn't make sense. When it was repeated, Joshi realised his mistake. It wasn't thunder, it was a spasm of coughing.

The whole log seemed to shake.

Wide-eyed, the three Quentarians turned and looked at each other.

'Run!' Joshi cried.

19

Goodbye
Kiss

ABELHA WAS RIGHT. THE smoke had made the bear very angry indeed. It came lumbering out of the log, roaring like a wounded dragon.

'Put the torch out!' hissed Abelha.

They were cowering behind a low thicket of ferns and bushes fifty feet from the mouth of the hollow log. There hadn't been time to go any farther and anyway Joshi was worried about hectapuses.

'I can't put it out,' he whispered. 'If the bear sees us, it's our only defence.'

In their rush to escape the waking bear, the other two had forgotten to bring flaming brands from the fire.

'But it will see us,' Abelha whispered urgently, 'if you don't extinguish the torch!'

She was right again. The huge bear turned in their direction. Baring its teeth and growling thunderously, it came stalking towards them like a small mountain range on legs.

Lying flat on the ground next to Joshi, Vindon slowly pulled his sword rattling from its scabbard. 'Here, couthin,' he whispered, offering it to Joshi. 'You'll need thith.'

Joshi pushed the weapon away. 'Keep your sword,' he said. 'You and Abelha might need it if something happens to me.'

Summoning all his courage, he scrambled to his feet and crept out from behind the bushes.

The huge animal let out a deafening bellow when it saw him, then rose up on its hind legs. It was so tall that the light from the flaming torch only reached halfway up its massive shaggy body, leaving its head in darkness. All Joshi could see above him were its eyes, glinting like distant stars. His every instinct told him to turn and run. *This shouldn't be happening to me!* he thought. *I'm just a gardener.*

But he wasn't a coward. Vindon's taunt still

echoed inside his head. *Beaten by a thirteen-year-old girl!* It was true — Taschia had beaten him. But she hadn't humbled him. Unlike his Uncle Terrak, Joshi hadn't run away. And he wasn't going to run away now.

Raising the guttering torch high above his head, Joshi let out the time-honoured Nibhelline battle cry and raced towards the giant bear.

The last thing the animal expected was to be attacked. Very likely it had never been attacked by anything in its whole life. While it was a cub its mother had protected it and when it matured the bear was the largest and most powerful creature in the forest — even the hectapuses were afraid of it. Yet now this puny little creature with one bright eye was rushing towards it, squealing like a hoarse parrot!

The bear was still groggy from sleep, both its eyes were swollen half-closed from bee stings and its throat was sore from the strange, evil-smelling clouds that had awoken it in its den. Somewhere in its sleep-fogged brain there was a dim memory of another bright eye like this one and that bright eye had hurt its nose. Was the parrot squeal a warning?

At the last moment, the giant bear stopped its

slow, swaying advance. The bright eye kept coming.
It blinded the bear to everything else around it.
There was just the bright eye and black darkness.
And the horrible parrot squeal! Confused, the great
bear spun around, dropped onto all fours and lum-
bered back towards the safety of its den.

But its retreat was blocked. Instead of a safe,
dark hollow, the bear encountered a dense bank of
the same evil-smelling clouds that had driven it out
in the first place. Worse, there was another bright
eye and this one was much larger — it seemed to fill
the whole den! With a roar of consternation, the
huge animal turned and charged blindly off into the
forest.

Joshi, Abelha and Vindon stood twenty feet back
from the mouth of the hollow log. It was as close as
they could get. The entrance was wreathed in
flames. Clouds of dense, pale smoke billowed out
into the night. The fire they had built to smoke the
bear out had spread — now the log itself was on fire.

It was Vindon who voiced the thoughts of all
three of them. 'We're never going to get back to
Quentarith now!'

Even though Joshi's reasoning told him this was so, he was not prepared to stand idly by while fate sealed his future. Shielding his face with one arm, he rushed forward and tried beating the flames out with a green branch, but the heat and the smoke soon drove him back. It was useless. The centuries-old wood was powdery and tinder dry — nothing could put it out. The whole log was going to burn away to nothing. The rift would disappear. They would be stuck in this world of giants for the rest of their lives. Not that the rest of their lives would be very long if the hectapuses and giant bears had anything to do with it, Joshi reflected sombrely.

Abelha gripped his arm. 'Joshi, I want you and Vindon to stay out of sight.'

'Why?' he asked, wondering why her hand was shivering.

'I think I know how to get back to the rift. But you'll have to promise to do exactly as I tell you,' she said. 'Do you promise, Joshi?'

He nodded. What choice did he have? 'I promise.'

'Good,' said the bee girl, releasing him. 'Hide behind those bushes. And don't come out — no matter what happens — until I tell you.'

Joshi looked at Vindon, who shrugged. 'Might

ath well,' Vindon said. 'Unleth you got any better
idea-th, couthin?'

Joshi had run right out of ideas. 'What are you
going to do, Abelha?'

She shook her head. Her eyes glistened in the
firelight. 'Just do what I say, Joshi. I think it'll
work.' Then she bobbed up on her toes and kissed
him on the lips. 'Go on,' she whispered, pushing
him gently in the direction of the bushes.

They crouched in the thicket, watching Abelha
through the leaves. 'What'th th-ee doing?' Vindon
asked.

'I don't know,' Joshi whispered. It was hard to
think clearly. Abelha had kissed him! Now she was
kneeling on the ground fifteen feet from the mouth
of the hollow log, illuminated by the dancing
yellow flames and the churning orange smoke that
billowed out of it like dragon's breath. And she
began to hum.

A shiver passed through Joshi. 'Look!' he gasped.

A faint yellow glow had appeared in the night
sky. Slowly it became brighter, lighting up the
forest canopy a thousand feet above them. There
was a roar like a great wind, then a blazing trail of
light descended through the threshing treetops as a
host of ghost bees came spiralling down. They were

so bright against the surrounding darkness that the two cousins had to shield their eyes.

Squinting through his fingers, Joshi watched as Abelha stood up and spread her arms to welcome the swirling storm of ghost bees. As they encircled her, the bee girl turned and walked slowly towards the mouth of the flaming log, leading the maelstrom of glowing bees behind her. Then she stepped right in! But the fire didn't harm her. The whirlwind of bees drew the smoke and the flames away, funnelling them harmlessly up into the sky. Within moments, the fire was extinguished and the log was clear of smoke.

'She's put the fire out!' cried Joshi. 'She's saved us!'

Vindon shook his head admiringly. 'Your girlfriend'th got a lot of gut-th, couthin,' he admitted. 'Thame th-ee'th got to die.'

'What?' gasped Joshi.

'They'll take her away now,' Vindon explained. 'Ghoth-t bee-th alway-th take thomething away.'

Finally everything made sense. Joshi realised why Abelha had been shaking. And why she'd kissed him. It had been a goodbye kiss. The bee girl had sacrificed herself so that he and Vindon could escape back to Quentaris.

Before Vindon could stop him, Joshi jumped to his feet and went crashing out of the bushes. He raced towards the log. But he was too late. Abelha had already stepped back out and the ghost bees swarmed all over her.

'Abelha!' he screamed. 'No-o-o-o-o-o-o-o-o-o!'

As the whirlwind of glowing bees spun her up into the night sky, the bee girl's tiny voice came floating down to Joshi through the roar of fifty thousand ghostly wings.

'Go, Joshi. Go home quickly! And look after my bees!'

But Joshi was unable to move. He stood rooted to the spot, his hands clawing at the empty black void above him, tears blinding his eyes.

'You heard her,' cried Vindon, grabbing his arm. 'We've got to go *now* — before the fire th-tart'th again.' And he tugged Joshi into the hollow log.

There was no time to lose. The ghost bees had blown out the flames, but the wood still smouldered and glowed all around them. For the first twenty feet it was like fire-walking. They dashed across glowing coals. It blistered Joshi's feet through his heavy gardener's boots. He heard Vindon muttering oaths of pain ahead of him. Then they were past the smouldering wood. And not a moment too soon. With a loud *whoosh*, the whole entrance burst into flame behind them. There was no going back now and no way that Abelha could follow if she managed to escape the ghost bees. Joshi tried to shut his mind to what had happened to her. She had given her life for his. If he died now, her sacrifice was for nothing. Eyes streaming tears, he stumbled after his cousin. They had no torch, but the wall of flames behind them lit up the whole log. Within a short time they reached the rift and squeezed through into another, more familiar world.

It was still daytime in Quentaris, though the sun was low in the sky. Gasping from smoke inhalation and squinting in the sudden glare of daylight, the two cousins staggered out of Deadly Cave.

And were met by a dozen burly, rough-looking men, with black bandannas tied round their heads and their swords drawn.

'Are you ready to die, lads?' the leader asked.

20

Quentaris's Most Wanted

IT WAS CAPTAIN HEMLOCK. Although this was the first time Joshi had laid eyes on him, the famous outlaw's handsome, unshaven face graced a thousand Wanted posters on noticeboards, walls and lamp-posts throughout Quentaris. Formerly an officer of the Rift Guard, Captain Hemlock had been dishonourably discharged for abandoning his post during a Zolka attack. Disgraced and out of work, the former soldier had turned robber, recruiting a gang of mercenaries, cut-throats and desperadoes who preyed on adventurers returning from other worlds, robbing them of any riches they had brought back with them and frequently taking their lives as well.

'Thpare uth, thir!' wailed Vindon, raising his trembling hands high above his head. 'We haven't got any treathure!'

'Ho, ho, ho! Th-o you didn't bring back any treathure, lad-th?' laughed Captain Hemlock, mimicking Vindon's lisp. Then his eyes became serious. 'Where have you been?'

'Nowhere you'd be interested in,' Joshi said.

The gang leader waved his sword threateningly. 'I'd be careful of my tone, lad, if I were you. Tell me where you've been.'

'It's a place where there isn't any treasure. There's only trees and scary animals.'

'Scary animals, hmmm. What happened to your friend's face?'

'Bee-th,' lisped Vindon. 'I wath th-tung by bee-th.'

Captain Hemlock raised an eyebrow. 'Thounds like a very th-cary place indeed!' he mocked, and several of his men laughed. He pointed his sword at Vindon. 'Drop your sword belt, lad.'

Without a word of protest this time, Vindon unbuckled his belt and let it fall to the ground.

'Now, would you both be so kind as to turn out your pockets.'

Joshi and Vindon obeyed, but the exercise produced nothing more valuable than a flint, a small piece of dragonwort root and three copper rounds.

'Looks like they're telling the truth, Captain,' one of the outlaws said. 'Might as well let them go.'

But the gang leader was eyeing Joshi closely. 'What's that stuck down your vest, squire?'

'Nothing,' Joshi lied.

With a deft flick of his sword, Captain Hemlock opened the front of Joshi's vest, sending the buttons flying. The long-stemmed skyflower fell to the dusty road.

'What's that?' demanded the outlaw.

'Just a flower.'

Captain Hemlock poked Joshi in the chest with his sword, forcing him to step backwards. He stooped and picked up the bedraggled flower. 'Green petals,' he said, and turned to his men. 'Ever heard of a green flower?'

They all shook their heads. 'Might be it's magic,' suggested one.

The gang leader looked Joshi in the eye. 'Is it?' he asked. 'Is this a magic flower?'

'No.'

'Is it valuable?'

'No.'

'Why did you bring it back then?'

Joshi shrugged. 'I like flowers.'

'Why is it,' mused Captain Hemlock, twirling the skyflower in his fingers, 'that I get the feeling you're lying? See, lad, I think there's something special about this flower that you're not telling me.'

'There isn't,' said Joshi. 'It's just a flower.'

'Then you won't have any objection if I keep it,' said Captain Hemlock, threading its stem into his bandanna above his right ear. Turning to his men, he asked, 'How do I look, lads?'

'Very dashing!'

'You look like a regular toff!'

'The ladies will be mad fer you now, Captain!'

Joshi stood perfectly still as the outlaws laughed and joked about the bedraggled green skyflower that stuck out at a jaunty angle above Captain Hemlock's ear. It's only a flower, he told himself, trying to remain calm. It isn't worth dying for.

But it was the single one of its kind in Quentaris. And he could never go back and get another one, now that the hollow log was on fire and the rift leading into the world of giants was about to be closed forever.

And Abelha had lost her life because of it.

Before he realised what he was doing, Joshi ducked down and scooped up Vindon's sword belt from the ground.

'Give it back!' he said, drawing the sword from its scabbard.

There was a moment of stunned silence. All twelve outlaws seemed to freeze; only their eyes moved, swivelling slowly round in their sockets and coming to rest on Joshi holding the sword.

'You fool!' Vindon whispered beside him. 'We're Zolka feed now!'

'Indeed you are!' vowed Captain Hemlock, over-hearing. Sword raised, the gang leader crunched towards them. There was a sparkle in his eyes. 'So you want your flower back, do you lad?' he said to Joshi. A cruel grin crept across his face. 'Let's see if you can take it from me, hmmm?'

The outlaws formed a circle, with Joshi and Captain Hemlock in the centre. Vindon, too, was part of the circle, an evil-looking dagger held to his throat. The gang leader faced Joshi, his well-oiled sword dangling almost casually from his right hand. But his eyes were focused and alert.

'Any time you're ready, lad.'

Vindon's right, Joshi thought, squaring up to his notorious opponent. I'm a fool and I'm going to die. But part of him didn't care. Without the skyflower, *and without Abelha*, he had nothing to live for. He was an embarrassment to his family, the butt of everyone's jokes, the only Nibhelline male who would rather grow flowers than wield a sword.

Well, he was wielding a sword now. *Take that!* he thought, swinging wildly at Captain Hemlock. The big outlaw jumped easily out of the way.

'Very nice piece of footwork, Captain!' one of the gang members commented.

'Why, thank you,' said the outlaw leader.

Joshi swung again, but Captain Hemlock easily parried his blow. The outlaw skipped in a circle, making no attempt to launch an attack of his own.

He's playing with me, Joshi thought, striking at him once more. There was a clash of steel as Captain Hemlock knocked his sword sideways so hard that Joshi nearly dropped it.

'Keep your guard up, lad,' advised the outlaw leader. 'You left yourself wide open there. I could have run you through.'

Why didn't you? Joshi wondered, squaring up to him again. He feinted a swing to the left, then twisted his wrists and nearly got his sword under the outlaw's blade. Captain Hemlock had to jump sharply backwards.

'Ho, ho! Got a few tricks up your sleeve, have you?' he laughed, and the green flower bobbed above his ear.

But Joshi didn't have any tricks left. His only lesson in sword fighting had come from a thirteen-year-old girl and she had taught *him* a lesson. If Abelha hadn't come along with her bees, it would have all ended then. Instead of now. This time the bee girl wasn't coming to Joshi's aid. She was dead. *Look after my bees!* were her last words to him. How could he possibly do that? He couldn't even look after himself!

Captain Hemlock's sword flashed in the late afternoon sunlight. Instinctively Joshi brought his own weapon up and steel clashed against steel. For a moment they were eye to eye, each straining to better the other as their swords locked, hilt to hilt. With a grunt, Joshi pushed the bigger man away. The outlaw staggered backwards and fell flat on his backside.

'*Touche!*' puffed Captain Hemlock, red-faced and sweating as he bounced back to his feet. 'Not much finesse, but the lad's got muscle.'

They circled each other. The outlaw's jaw was set and the sparkle was gone from his eyes. *He means to finish this soon*, Joshi realised with a shiver of apprehension.

Then he saw the bee.

It buzzed twice around the outlaw's head, then settled on the skyflower. Its weight bent the stem down so that both flower and bee dangled in Captain Hemlock's eye. The outlaw flinched and swiped at the insect. And in that moment of distraction, Joshi struck.

None of those watching saw the bee. To the onlookers, it appeared that the boy won the fight fair and square. His attack was lightning fast. Distracted by the insect, Captain Hemlock saw Joshi's flashing sword only at the very last moment. For a split second he contemplated bringing his own weapon up, but realised it was too late to make a defensive move. Instead, he relaxed his right hand and allowed the sword to drop from his fingers as the tip of Joshi's sword pressed against his throat.

'Nice move,' gasped the outlaw leader, raising both hands in surrender.

'Kneel down,' Joshi commanded.

Captain Hemlock dropped to his knees. All around them, eleven swords slid from their scabbards.

'Tell your men,' Joshi said loudly, 'that if they don't drop their swords, I'll slit your throat.'

'He's bluffing,' said Captain Hemlock.

'Try me!' Joshi warned, his eyes locked on the outlaw leader's, his sword pressed against his windpipe.

Captain Hemlock took a deep breath. His Adam's apple wobbled. 'Do as the lad says,' he gasped.

One by one, the outlaws dropped their swords.

'Everyone step back,' Joshi ordered. 'Vindon, grab all their swords.'

'Now what are we going to do?' Vindon asked when he had gathered the outlaws' weapons. The eleven gang members stood in a big circle around them, glowering and flexing their fists.

Not for a moment did Joshi take his eyes off Captain Hemlock, nor the sword from the outlaw's throat. With his free hand, he plucked the skyflower from above Captain Hemlock's ear.

'We wait for the cavalry,' he said.

From the direction of the city below them, came the clatter of galloping hooves.

Commander Storm had never made an easier arrest. She had been leading a mounted patrol on a routine visit to the Last and First Station, when a guard on the main gate reported a skirmish of some kind up near one of the rift caves. Riding up to investigate, Commander Storm had come upon Quentaris's Most

Wanted outlaw, Captain Hemlock, in the custody of two heavily armed youths. The rest of his gang outnumbered the mounted officers two to one, but without their weapons they put up little resistance and Commander Storm's men soon rounded them up.

'Don't I know you two?' The commander of the City Watch frowned at Joshi and Vindon as the outlaws were led away. 'You're the gardener, aren't you? And you're Terrak's boy. Well, well, well, it's nice to see you've settled your differences and decided to use your, er, aggressive tendencies where they most benefit society. Nice work, by the way. Did you know there's a reward of fifty royals for capturing Captain Hemlock?'

The cousins looked at each other.

'I gueth you thould get the reward, Jothi,' Vindon said, the expression on his swollen face an odd mixture of envy and admiration. 'After everything you've done.'

Joshi handed his sword back. 'No Vindon, we had an agreement. We'll split the money,' he said.

His share would go to Abelha's family and they could use part of it to hire a beekeeper to tend her hives. All Joshi wanted was the skyflower.

21

The Seed

JOSHI PUSHED THE TINY seed deep into the rich, black earth. It was beautiful soil. Drass had spared no expense in preparing the two tastefully landscaped garden beds that now graced the front of Nibhelline Manor. He had followed Joshi's every direction to the letter, ordering cartloads of peat moss from Hadran, sand from the Barrenlands, fish fertiliser from the river traders, dung from Malodour the pig farmer and mulch from the forests of Simesia. People had laughed at first (though never out loud) to see the proud, powerful and somewhat overweight Head of House Nibhelline bent over a garden pike beside the now famous young Green who had bested Captain Hemlock, but the two of them were invariably so deep in conversation about flowers, compost and horticulture that they didn't notice. Nor did Joshi notice (or he pretended not to) the admiring glances he received from almost every young lady who found an excuse to linger for a few minutes outside Nibhelline Manor, pretending to admire the flourishing gardens.

So the soft female voice behind him didn't register at first as Joshi covered the precious seed with soil and sprinkled water on it from a wooden bucket.

'It won't flower for a hundred years, you realise.'

It was the words, rather than the voice that had uttered them, that registered in Joshi's mind. She was right. Plants rarely flowered until they were mature and a thousand-foot tree would take years to mature. Probably much *more* than a century.

'Skyfire!' he muttered, sitting back on his heels in the warm black earth.

A bee buzzed around him. Joshi didn't wave it away. He liked bees now and he had no fear of them. In fact, there was very little that he was afraid of.

'What am I going to tell Drass?' he sighed.

'Tell him,' the voice said softly, 'that his grandchildren will have something to look forward to.

156

And so might *ours.*'

Joshi froze. There were several bees flying around him now. And a steady, rising hum behind him. He stood up so quickly that he knocked the bucket over.

'Abelha!'

'Hullo, flower boy,' she said, and rushed into his arms.

They hugged each other. It was several minutes before either of them said another word. Two young ladies, who just happened to be promenading past Nibhelline Manor in their Highday finery (even though it was only Leshday), turned quickly and marched away with downcast eyes and small, pinched mouths.

Joshi recovered his voice finally, but he found it difficult to speak. 'I thought you were … How did you … ?'

'I don't remember much,' Abelha said, dusting a speck of pollen off his cheek. 'I think some of the ghost bees remembered me. So they brought me home.'

'I'm …' Joshi was still having difficulty accepting that the bee girl was real. That she was back. That she was *alive!* 'I'm … glad.'

'You're *glad!*' Abelha said, pretending to take offence. 'Is that the best you can do, flower boy?'

'No, bee girl,' he said mischievously. 'You can try *this*, for starters.'

And for a long time, the only sound to be heard in Drass Nibhelline's pristine green garden was the joyful humming of bees.

Stolen Children of Quentaris

Gary Crew

Why did Nordian traders kidnap children from the city of Quentaris? Did they really sell them to the hideous Rodentia, rat king of the Trollantan Mountains? In this spellbinding prequel to *The Plague of Quentaris*, best-selling author Gary Crew reveals all ...

Gary Crew is one of Australia's most awarded authors, winning the Children's Book Council of Australia Book of the Year four times. He is internationally acclaimed for his fantasy novels and illustrated books.

0 7344 0880 3

Pirates of Quentaris

Sherryl Clark

Kiall and Eena's father has been thrown in prison for failure to repay merchants for goods lost in a series of disastrous shipwrecks. Desperate to save him, their only option is to go fortune-hunting in the rift caves — but they can't afford a guide. Kiall decides to sneak onto a pirate ship and travel through the caves. If he can just steal gold from the pirates and bring it back, all will be saved ...

Sherryl Clark has been writing stories and poems for more than twenty years. Her first children's book, *The Too-Tight Tutu*, was a best-selling Aussie Bite. Her other titles include more Aussie Bites, Nibbles and Chomps such as *The Littlest Pirate*, *Boots and All* and *Batter Up*. She has also written the novels *Up a Tree* and *Flipside* for older readers. Her verse novel, *Farm Kid*, won the 2005 NSW Premier's Patricia Wrightson prize for children's literature.

0 7344 0883 8

Stars of Quentaris

Michael Pryor

A missing star? A fabulous reward? Nisha and Tal are ready for adventure! With the well-meaning assistance of Tal's musical mentor, Esbandalon, Nisha and Tal are matched against hordes of other treasure seekers, in a helter-skelter race to find a missing celestial visitor. But first they must face pursuit by Voiceless Rin and his brigade of ruffians.

Michael Pryor is the popular author of many award-winning novels and short stories, including *Quentaris in Flames, Beneath Quentaris, Stones of Quentaris* and *Nightmare in Quentaris*. Michael lives in Melbourne with his wife Wendy and two daughters, Celeste and Ruby.

0 7344 0881 1

The Forgotten Prince

Paul Collins

Thieves' Guild apprentice Crocodile Sal is sitting her prac exam, Deceit and Daring 101. Her goal is to find a job and stay in it for at least three months. During this time, she has to steal something really valuable and use it in a successful, diabolical crime. Simple enough. But she hasn't reckoned on royal and political intrigue, assassins, shape-shifters, betrayal, kidnapping gypsies, rift-world travel, trolls and murderous swamp creatures. Can anything else go wrong?

Paul Collins has been short-listed for many Australian science fiction and fantasy awards, and has won the Aurealis, William Atheling and inaugural Peter McNamara awards. His books include *The Great Ferret Race, The Earthborn, Dragonlinks, Swords of Quentaris, Slaves of Quentaris, Dragonlords of Quentaris* and *Princess of Shadows*.

0 7344 0882 X

Prisoner of Quentaris

Anna Ciddor

'I know of a land of giants, where one man could wipe out all the people in leprechaun land with a single sneeze,' boasts Heaney.

He soon regrets his words, for when Finnegan, king of the leprechauns, ventures through the rift caves to see this dangerous land for himself, he is taken prisoner by the giants! Heaney and the other leprechauns set out in a valiant attempt to rescue their king. But can these tiny warriors possibly overpower the mighty giants of Quentaris?

Anna Ciddor is one of Australia's most popular and acclaimed writers for younger readers, with books published around the world. Her best-selling Viking Magic trilogy, comprising the books *Runestone*, *Wolfspell* and *Stormriders*, has been short-listed for numerous awards. *Runestone* was selected as a Notable Book by the Children's Book Council of Australia in 2003.

0 7344 0887 0